QUICKSAND

Junichirō Tanizaki was born in 1886 in Tokyo, where his family owned a printing establishment. He studied Japanese literature at Tokyo Imperial University, and his first published work, a one-act play, appeared in 1910 in a literary magazine he helped to found. Tanizaki lived in the cosmopolitan Tokyo area until the earthquake of 1923, when he moved to the gentler and more cultivated Kyoto-Osaka region, the scene of *The Makioka Sisters*. There he became absorbed in the Japanese past and abandoned his superficial Westernization. All his most important works were written after 1923, among them *Naomi* (1924), *Some Prefer Nettles* (1929), *Arrowroot* (1931), *Ashikari (The Read Cutter)* (1932), *A Portrait of Shunkin* (1932), *The Secret History of the Lord of Musashi* (1935), several modern versions of *The Tale of Genji* (1941, 1954 and 1965), *The Makioka Sisters* (1943–48), *Captain Shigemoto's Mother* (1949), *The Key* (1956), and *Dairy of a Mad Old Man* (1961). By 1930 he had gained such renown that an edition of his complete works was published, and he was awarded an Imperial Award for Cultural Merit in 1949. In 1964 he was elected an honorary Member of the American Academy and the National Institute of Arts and Letters, the first Japanese to receive this honour. Tanizaki died in 1965.

The translator of *Quicksand*, Howard Hibbett, is Victor S. Thomas Professor of Japanese Literature, Emeritus, at Harvard University. He has also translated Tanizaki's *Diary of a Mad Old Man* and *The Key*. He lives in Arlington, Massachusetts.

D1339298

ALSO BY JUNICHIRŌ TANIZAKI

Junichirō Tanizaki

QUICKSAND

TRANSLATED BY
Howard Hibbett

VINTAGE

Published by Vintage 2000

2 4 6 8 10 9 7 5 3 1

This translation is based on the ChuoKoron Sha, Inc.
edition of *Manji*, published in Japan in 1947. *Manji* was
serialized in *Kaizo* in 1928-30

First published in Great Britain by Vintage 1994
First published in the United States by
Alfred A. Knopf in 1994

Vintage
Random House, 20 Vauxhall Bridge Road,
London SW1V 2SA

Random House Australia (Pty) Limited
20 Alfred Street, Milsons Point, Sydney
New South Wales 2061, Australia

Random House New Zealand Limited
18 Poland Road, Glenfield,
Auckland 10, New Zealand

Random House (Pty) Limited
Endulini, 5A Jubilee Road, Parktown 2193,
South Africa

The Random House Group Limited Reg. No. 954009
www.randomhouse.co.uk

A CIP catalogue record for this book
is available from the British Library

ISBN 0 09 948561 3

Printed and bound in Great Britain by
The Guernsey Press Co. Ltd., Guernsey, Channel Islands

Quicksand

1

DO FORGIVE ME for bothering you again, but I simply *had* to see you today—I want you to hear my side of the story, from beginning to end. Are you sure you don't mind? I know how busy you are with your own writing, and if I go into every last detail it might take forever! Really, I only wish I could put it all down on paper, like one of your novels, and ask you to read it. . . . The truth is, the other day I tried to start writing, but what happened is so *complicated* I didn't know where to begin. So I thought I'd just have to talk it out, and that's why I'm here. But then, I hate to let you waste your precious time for my sake. Are you quite sure it's all right? You've always been so sweet to me I'm afraid I'm taking advantage of your kindness, and after everything you've put up with . . . I can't thank you enough.

Well, I suppose I ought to start with that man I used to talk so much about. As I told you before, what you said made me think the whole thing over, and I finally broke off with him. Still, I must have felt a strong attachment. Even at home I'd get almost hysterical when anything brought him to mind. But before long it began to dawn on me that the man was worthless. . . . My husband noticed I'd changed completely since I began consulting you. Instead of always rushing off, telling him I was going to a concert or something, I would stay in all day painting or practicing the piano.

"You're being more feminine lately," he used to say. I could see he was pleased by your concern.

But I have to admit I never said a word to him about the other man. "It isn't healthy to hide your past mistakes from your husband," you warned me, "and since you tell me you haven't already gone too far up till now, why not make a clean breast of it?" And yet . . . I suppose even my husband may have had an inkling about what was going on, but somehow it was hard for me to confess. I told myself I'd just try not to make the same mistake over again, and I kept that love affair a secret hidden deep in my heart. So he didn't really know what we were talking about, you see; he thought you were simply giving me a lot of good advice. It's made a wonderful change in your attitude, he said.

▼

For a while I spent my time quietly at home. Perhaps because he felt relieved, the way things were going, he said he'd better get a little more serious himself, so he rented an office in the Imabashi Building in downtown Osaka and opened a law practice. That was early last year; it must have been around February.

. . . Yes, that's right: he studied German law at the university and could have become a lawyer anytime he liked. But it seems he wanted to be a professor, and he was in graduate school at the time I was involved with that other man. There was no special reason why he decided to go into practice. Probably he was ashamed of depending on my parents and felt he couldn't hold his head up before me. He'd had such a splendid record as a student that my parents considered him a prize catch. When we were married, they took him into the family like an adopted son. They trusted him right from the start and settled some property on us so he needn't be in any hurry about making a living. Since he wanted to be a legal scholar, let him keep on studying and be one. And we could go abroad together for two or three years, if we cared to.

At first my husband was delighted and seemed to mean to do just that. But then maybe I began to irritate him; maybe he thought I was entirely too willful, because of my family's position. Anyway, he simply didn't know how to get along with people, no matter what, and he was so tactless, so blunt, that after he started to practice law he still had hardly any business. Yet he made a point of going to the office every day, and I was left to lounge around the house from morning till night. Naturally all those fading memories began coming to life again. Before, when I had time on my hands I used to write poetry, but that would only have stirred up even more memories. So it seemed to me I couldn't go on like that; I had to take up something, find *some* distraction. . . .

Perhaps you know that Women's Arts Academy in

the Tennoji district? It's a third-rate private school, with departments for painting, music, sewing, embroidery, and all. They have no such thing as admission requirements—anyone can get in, adults or children. I'd had some lessons in Japanese-style painting and was still fond of it, though I wasn't very good, so I began going there every day, leaving in the morning with my husband. I say every day, but of course it was the kind of school where you could always take the day off.

My husband had not the slightest interest in art or literature, but he was quite willing to have me go to school. He even encouraged me, told me it was a fine idea, I should do my best! Although we usually left the house together in the morning, we went whenever I was ready—sometimes nine o'clock, sometimes ten—but things were so quiet at my husband's office that he would wait for me as long as I pleased. We'd take the Hanshin train in from Koroen to Umeda, then catch a taxi and drive along the Sakai streetcar line to the corner of Imabashi, where I dropped him off. I'd go on by taxi all the way to Tennoji.

He enjoyed our going out together like that.

"I feel as if I'm a student again," he'd say, in high spirits, and laugh when I remarked: "Would a student couple run back and forth to school by taxi?"

He wanted me to call him when I was ready to leave in the afternoon too, and stop by his office, or meet him at Namba or the Hanshin station, to go to the movies at the Shochiku Theater or somewhere. That was how things stood. We were getting along very well. But then, maybe about the middle of April, I had a stupid quarrel with the director at my school.

▼

It's strange, the way it happened. You know, they use models posed in various costumes for Japanese painting—you never work from the nude—and there was a so-called life class of that kind at the school. Just then they had a Miss Y, an eighteen-year-old girl said to be one of the most beautiful models in Osaka, and they had her pose in a gauzy white robe as the Willow Kannon—well, that was supposed to be close enough to naked to qualify as life study.

So I was sketching her one day, along with the other students, when the director came into the classroom and said to me:

"Mrs. Kakiuchi, your picture doesn't look anything like the model. Possibly you have a different model in mind?"

Then he gave a sort of mocking laugh, and all the rest of the students saw what was going on and began to snicker too. I was startled and felt myself blush, though at the time I had no idea why. Thinking back on it now, I'm not sure I *was* blushing, but somehow his remark about "a different model" struck home. Who could the model be? It seems that quite unconsciously, as I was looking at Miss Y there before me, I'd had another distinct image in my mind's eye. That image was reflected in the drawing—my brush seemed to be sketching it all by itself, without any intention on my part.

I'm sure you know who I mean. My model—it's all been in the newspapers anyway—was Miss Tokumitsu Mitsuko.

▼

(*Author's note:* The widow Kakiuchi seemed unaffected by her recent ordeal. Her dress and manner were bright, even showy, just as they had been a year before. Rather than a widow, Mrs. Kakiuchi looked like the typical young married Osaka woman of good family, and she spoke in the mellifluous feminine dialect of her class and region. She was certainly no great beauty, but as she said the name "Tokumitsu Mitsuko," her face became suffused with a curious radiance.)

▼

At that time I hadn't yet made friends with Mitsuko. She was studying oil painting—painting in the Western style, that is—so she was in a different classroom, and there was no chance for us to talk. I didn't think she would even recognize me or would give me a second thought if she did. Not that I paid any special attention to her either, except that she seemed to be a strikingly attractive girl. Of course we'd scarcely said a word to each other, and I didn't know the first thing about her temperament, what she was really like. I suppose you could say it was just a general impression.

Come to think of it, though, she must have been on my mind a good deal earlier, since already, without even asking, I knew Mitsuko's name and where she lived: she was the daughter of a wholesale woolens merchant whose shop was in the Semba district of Osaka, and now they lived out in Ashiya, along the Hankyu line—things like that. So when the director made his snide little remark, it set me thinking. Yes, the face in my sketch looked like Mitsuko, but it wasn't something I'd done on purpose. Even if I *had*, why should I be expected to produce a facial likeness of Miss Y? She was posing as the goddess Kannon so that we could study her figure, the drapery folds of her white robe, and all that, and then just try to express the feeling of a Kannon bodhisattva, surely. Miss Y may have been a beautiful model, but Mitsuko was far more beautiful: as long as it enhanced the portrait, what was wrong with modeling the face after Mitsuko's? That was what I thought.

2

TWO OR THREE DAYS later the director came in again while we were sketching the same pose. He stopped in front of me and stared at my work with his usual sneering smile.

"Mrs. Kakiuchi," he said. "Really now, Mrs. Kakiuchi, there's something wrong with your picture. It's looking less and less like the model. Who exactly *are* you modeling it on?"

"Oh, is that so?" I answered sharply. "It doesn't look at all like the model?" As if the director had anything to do with teaching art!

... No, the regular painting teacher wasn't there. That would have been Professor Tsutsui Shunko, but he came in only occasionally, to tell us this or that was bad, or to do it a different way; ordinarily the students would just look at the model and draw anyhow they pleased. I'd heard that the director taught English, one of the optional courses, but he didn't seem to have a

college degree or any real academic background; no
one even knew where he had gone to school. As I
found out afterward, he was no educator, just a shrewd
businessman. A man like that could hardly be expected
to understand painting, and he had no reason to stick
his nose into it. Then, too, most courses were left to
the specialists who taught them, so he rarely visited a
classroom. And yet he went out of his way to come to
this class and criticize my painting!

Then he asked me in a sarcastic tone: "Now, seriously, you don't really think you're following that
model, do you?"

I pretended to be innocent. "Yes. I'm afraid I can't
draw very well, so maybe it isn't turning out right. But
I'm trying to be faithful."

"No," he said, "it's not that you can't draw. You're
rather talented, in fact. But look at this face—I can't help
thinking it's somebody else." He was back to that again.

"Oh, you're talking about the face, are you?" I said.
"That's to express my own ideal."

"And who might your ideal be?" he persisted tire-
somely.

Then I told him: "It's an ideal, not any special person. I just want to make the face beautiful, to give the
pure feeling of a Kannon. Is anything wrong with that?
Do I have to make even the *face* look like that model?"

"You're putting up quite an argument," he replied.
"But if you're capable of expressing your ideal, you
have no reason to come to this school. Isn't that why we
have you sketch from a model? You don't need a model
if you're going to paint any way you want, and if this

ideal Kannon of yours looks like somebody else, I think you're being pretty deceitful."

"I'm not a bit deceitful! And I don't see anything wrong artistically, as long as it has the divine features of a Kannon."

"It just won't do," he insisted. "You're not yet a full-fledged artist. Even if it seems divine to you, the question is how others see it. That sort of thing leads to misunderstanding."

"Oh? And what kind of misunderstanding might that be?" I retorted. "You're always saying it looks like someone, so would you please tell me who it looks like!"

That rattled him. "Stubborn, aren't you?" he said. From then on, the director held his tongue.

▼

I was elated. Facing down the director made me feel as if I had won a quarrel. But our argument in front of the students caused a sensation, and before long a nasty rumor began to spread. They said I'd made indecent advances to Mitsuko, that Mitsuko and I were altogether too close. . . . As I told you, at that time I'd hardly said a word to her, so the whole thing was nonsense, just an out-and-out lie. Of course I was aware that people were talking behind my back, though I never dreamed they were making such a fuss. But I had nothing on my conscience, so I didn't care what they said. It was all perfectly ridiculous.

Well, that's the way people are—they're always ready to spread rumors. Still, no matter how much they gossiped, to accuse us of being "altogether too close" when we'd had nothing to do with each other was so absurd that it didn't even make me angry. I wasn't concerned for myself—what bothered me was how Mitsuko might take it. It occurred to me that she must be distressed to be drawn into all this, and somehow whenever our paths crossed, going to school or leaving, I couldn't bring myself to look her in the face the way I used to. And yet to speak up and apologize to her—that might make things worse, cause even more scandal, and that wouldn't do either. Every time I happened to pass her I tried to seem apologetic, cringing and casting my eyes down, as if I wanted to escape her notice. All the same, I still felt anxious about whether she might be angry, or how she might look at me, so the moment we passed I would steal a glance at her. But Mitsuko's expression was the same as ever; she didn't seem in the least annoyed with me.

Oh yes, I've brought along a photograph I'd like to show you. We had it taken of us together when we got our matching kimonos—it's the one that was in the papers and attracted so much attention. As you can see, standing side by side like this I'm just a foil for Mitsuko; you won't find another such dazzling beauty among all the young girls around Semba.

▼

(*Author's note:* The "matching kimonos" in the photograph were of the gaudy, colorful sort that is so much to the Osaka taste. Mrs. Kakiuchi wore her hair pulled back in a chignon; Mitsuko's was done up in a traditional Shimada, but her eyes were rich, liquid, extraordinarily passionate for a young city-bred girl of Osaka. In short, the eyes were fascinating, full of the magnetic power of a love goddess. Certainly she was very beautiful; there was no false modesty in the widow's remark about being a foil for her. But whether her face was in fact suitable for the benign features of the Willow Kannon was perhaps another matter.)

▼

But what do *you* think? An elaborate Japanese hairstyle is quite becoming to her, don't you agree?

. . . Yes, she sometimes wore it that way even to school. She said her mother liked her in it. Anyway, it was the kind of school that didn't require students to wear a uniform, and nobody cared if you had a Japanese coiffure or wore a plain kimono with no hakama skirt; whatever you liked. I never wore a hakama myself. Now and then Mitsuko came in Western clothes, but when she dressed in Japanese style it was always just a kimono. In this picture her hairdo makes her look several years younger, though actually she was twenty-two, only a year younger than myself—if she were still alive now, in 1928, she'd be twenty-three this year. But Mitsuko was an inch or two taller, and a beauty like that, even if she doesn't mean to be vain, always seems to have a confident air, doesn't she? Or maybe that's just my own sense of inferiority. Even later, after we were close, I always felt a little deferential toward her, like her younger sister, in spite of being the older one.

Well, around that time—to go back to when we'd hardly spoken, that is—it seemed that Mitsuko hadn't heard those nasty rumors I mentioned, since there wasn't the slightest change in her attitude. I had long ago been attracted by her beauty, and before the rumors started I used to edge near her whenever she came by. Mitsuko herself always walked straight on, as if she didn't even see me, but everything around seemed brighter and fresher after she passed. If she had heard those rumors, she would at least have paid some attention to me, I thought. I'd have noticed something in her manner, whether she loathed me or felt sorry for me, but there wasn't a hint of her feelings, so little by little I grew bolder, bold enough to edge near and peep into that lovely face again. One day during the lunch break we ran into each other in the student lounge, and instead of going coolly by, as usual, for some reason she gave me an enchanting smile. Instinctively I bowed, and then Mitsuko came up to me and said:

"I'm terribly sorry for all the trouble I've caused you. Please don't hold it against me."

"Whatever are you saying?" I replied. "I'm the one to apologize."

"You have nothing to apologize for. If you only knew what's going on . . . Be careful, someone's trying to trap us!"

"Really? Who could that be?" I asked.

"It's the director," she said. "I can't explain here— shall we go out somewhere for lunch? Then you can hear all about it."

"I'll go anywhere you like," I told her.

After that the two of us went to a restaurant near Tennoji Park. As we were eating lunch, Mitsuko began by saying that it was the director himself who started those malicious rumors. Of course I'd found it irritating, the way he kept coming into the classroom and embarrassing me before everyone, and I couldn't help feeling he was up to no good. But when I asked why on earth he wanted to spread a rumor like that, she said that the whole thing was aimed at *her*, that one way or another he wanted to damage her reputation. And the reason for *that* was talk of a marriage proposal, a proposal from the young man who was heir to the fortune of the M family, one of the richest and most famous families in Osaka.

Mitsuko said that she herself wasn't interested, but her own family was very much in favor of the match, and the other party seemed equally eager to have her. But apparently the daughter of a certain municipal councilman had also been offered for marriage to this Mr. M, which meant that she was in competition with Mitsuko. Even though Mitsuko had no desire to be a rival, the councilman's family must have felt they were up against a formidable enemy. Anyway, the young Mr. M was enthralled by Mitsuko's beauty and had even sent her love letters, so no doubt she *was* a formidable enemy.

Now the councilman's people were bustling about, doing their best to find some flaw in Mitsuko, and had tried everything they could think of, even spreading lies about involvement with another man; not content, they had finally turned to bribing the director of our school. Oh yes, and before that—this is getting to be hopelessly confused, I'm afraid—sometime before that, she said, the director had asked her father if he couldn't lend the school a thousand yen, to repair the building. Mitsuko's family had so much money that a thousand yen meant nothing to them, and they might have listened to an open request for a donation. But asking for a loan was strange enough, in the first place, and you couldn't begin to repair a building that size for a thousand yen. It all seemed so nonsensical that her father flatly refused. According to Mitsuko, the director often called on the families of students who were well off, asking for loans like that, but had never once returned any borrowed money. If he'd used the money properly it would have been different, but he let things run down till the building was just a pigsty, a dilapidated one at that!

. . . What? No, it seems he used all that money for personal expenses. She said the director was a real expert at toadying to wealthy students; and then there was his wife, the school's embroidery teacher: those two were always arranging little Sunday outings to curry favor. Actually, it was quite extravagant, the way they lived. If you lent them money they were very friendly, but if you refused them they would say unpleasant things about you behind your back. In Mitsuko's case, they not only had that grudge against her, they'd also been approached by the councilman, so there was no limit to the kind of thing they'd stoop to.

"That's why they used you to trap me, you see," Mitsuko said.

"To think there was all that behind it! I had no idea. It's so ridiculous, isn't it, when you and I didn't really know each other until today. Making up a story like that is bad enough, but I can't imagine anybody believing it."

"That's why you're easily taken in," Mitsuko replied. "People are saying it's only because of the rumors that we don't talk to each other at school. Why, someone even claimed they saw us getting on the train to Nara together last Sunday."

I was appalled. "Now who would say a thing like that?"

"Apparently it came from the director's wife. They're a great deal craftier than you think—so do be careful!"

3

WELL, MITSUKO kept begging me to forgive her, repeating how sorry she was, and that made me feel all the more sympathetic. "No, no, you haven't done anything wrong," I said to console her. "It's that dreadful man. And he's supposed to be an educator! . . . But it doesn't matter what they say about me—you're young and not yet married, so don't let yourself be victimized by such spiteful people!"

"I'm glad I had a chance to tell you the whole story. It's taken a weight off my mind." Then she smiled. "But if we meet again like this there'll be more gossip, so maybe we'd better not."

"What a shame, now that we've finally become friends!" Somehow the thought really bothered me.

"I do want to be your friend, if it's all right with you," Mitsuko said. "Next time, won't you come to my house? I'm not a bit afraid of what people say."

"And I'm not afraid either. If the gossip gets

too bad, I'll just stop going to that miserable school."

"Listen, Kakiuchi-san, I have an idea. Wouldn't you just love to make fun of everyone by showing them what good friends we are? How does that appeal to you?"

"It's fine with me," I said, "and I'd like to see the director's face when we do." I was quite taken with the notion.

"And this would be fun too!" said Mitsuko, clapping her hands like a mischievous child. "How about actually going to Nara together this Sunday?"

"Yes, let's do it! Just think of what they'll say when they hear *that*!"

And so, within less than an hour, we had thrown off the last trace of reserve between us.

By then it was much too late to go back to school, and one of us suggested seeing a movie at the Shochiku. We spent the rest of the afternoon together, until Mitsuko announced that she had some shopping to do and walked off along Shinsaibashi. I took a taxi from Nippombashi to the Imabashi office. As usual, I called for my husband and we went to the Hanshin station for the train home.

But this time he remarked: "You seem all excited today. What happened to make you look so cheerful?"

Do I really? I thought to myself. Is that all because of Mitsuko?

"Well," I said, "today I made a marvelous new friend."

"And who would that be?"

"A real beauty, that's who! You know that woolens merchant Tokumitsu in Semba? She's their daughter."

"How did you get to know her?"

"She goes to my school—the fact is, somebody started an ugly rumor about us. . . ." I had nothing to hide, so I told him everything, beginning with that silly argument I'd had with the director.

"What a school!" my husband said. "But if she's so beautiful, I'd like to meet her myself," he added jokingly.

"I'm sure she'll be visiting us soon. I promised to go to Nara with her next Sunday, if that's all right."

"Of course." My husband laughed. "I warn you, you'll make the director angry!"

▼

At school the next day, word had already got around about our lunch together and our going to the movies. There were all sorts of catty comments—you know how women are.

"You were strolling along Dotombori yesterday, weren't you, Kakiuchi-san?"

"You must have been having fun."

"Who could that have been with you?"

But Mitsuko enjoyed it and deliberately came over to me, as if to flaunt our friendship. Things went on like that for two or three days, by which time we were fast friends. The director seemed furious, but only glowered at us and didn't say a word. Mitsuko asked if I couldn't make my Kannon portrait look even more like her. "I wonder what he'd say then." So I tried to make the resemblance closer, but the director stopped coming into the classroom altogether. That delighted us.

We really needn't have gone to Nara, but since it happened to be a lovely late-April Sunday, I phoned her and arranged to meet at the Ueroku terminus, and we spent the afternoon wandering around the gentle slopes of Mount Wakakusa. Sophisticated as she was, there was still something childlike about Mitsuko, and when we got to the top she bought half a dozen tangerines and began rolling them down the hill, crying out: "Watch this!" The tangerines would roll on and on, down to the bottom; one of them even jumped across the road and through the open gate of a house on the other side. She seemed to find it all very amusing.

"Mitsuko, how about gathering some bracken?" I suggested. "I know there's a lot of bracken and horsetail on the next hill." We stayed till evening, picking quantities of bracken and flowering ferns and horsetail.

. . . Where were we on Mount Wakakusa? It has three peaks, you know, and we were in the hollow between the first two—you can see young herbs all over; they're especially delicious because the dead grass is burned off every spring. Anyway, it had begun to get dark by the time we came back over the first hill, and we were both so tired that we sat down to rest for a while when we were about halfway down the slope.

Suddenly Mitsuko looked serious.

"Kakiuchi-san, there's something I want to thank you for." When I asked her what that could be, she smiled knowingly and said: "Well, thanks to you, it looks as if I won't have to marry that horrid man."

"Really? And how did that happen?"

"Rumors get around fast. Those people have already heard all about you and me."

4

"I HAD TO LISTEN to the same thing at home last night," Mitsuko went on. "My mother took me aside and asked about that rumor circulating at school—was it true? There was a rumor, all right, I said, but how did you hear about it, Mother? That doesn't matter, she insisted; just tell me whether or not it's true. I admitted that you and I were good friends—what was wrong with that? For a moment she seemed at a loss. Well, now, there's nothing wrong with being good friends, she said, but aren't they accusing you of something improper? When I asked her what *that* meant, Mother replied that she didn't know anything more, but still there must be some reason why the rumor started. Oh, now I understand, I said. My friend liked my looks enough to use me as her model, and after that everybody began to shun us. That school is full of busybodies; if you're even a little pretty they say spiteful things about you—so yes, I can see how that kind of talk might get started. My mother was beginning to be convinced. Then it's not your fault, she said, but I wouldn't be too close to that Mrs. So-and-so. You've got to be awfully careful about your reputation, especially at this stage in your life, so don't let yourself in for foolish gossip. And that was the end of that. Obviously the councilman's people got word of the rumor and passed it on to M and his family, before my mother heard it. So I'm sure she thinks the marriage plans are off."

That made me uneasy.

"I know you must be pleased," I said, "but what about your mother? Just wait; she'll probably tell you to have nothing to do with me. I'd hate to give her the wrong idea about us."

"You needn't worry," Mitsuko assured me. "I've thought of telling her all about that greedy director, who tries to be so clever—about how he goes around talking behind your back if you won't lend him money and how he was bribed by the councilman. But I haven't. I'm afraid she might make me stop going to such an awful school, and then I wouldn't be able to see you."

"You're pretty clever yourself, aren't you!"

"Well, maybe I do know a thing or two," Mitsuko said, with a giggle. "If you don't fight fire with fire, it's your loss."

"Anyway, if your marriage talks have broken off, the councilman's daughter must be happy."

"Then both of us should thank you!"

▼

We kept on chatting there for over an hour. I'd been up Mount Wakakusa often but had never stayed until dusk, so it was really the first time I saw that broad landscape bathed in the evening haze. Until only a little while before, a few people had been lingering on the hillside, but by now, all the way down from the summit, there wasn't a soul. Quite a crowd had been out that day, so the green hillside was littered with tangerine peels, sake bottles, and other picnic leavings. Although the sky still had a twilight glow, you could see the city lights of Nara glimmering below us; in the distance, just across the valley, the lights of the Mount Ikoma cable car stretched in a long arc like a rosary, flickering in and out of view through the purple haze. As I gazed at those flickering lights I had a kind of choking feeling, and Mitsuko said: "My, it's already evening. It seems so lonely."

"I'm glad I'm *not* alone—I'd be scared to death!"

Mitsuko sighed. "If you're with someone you love, a lonely place like this is just right."

As long as I'm with you I could stay here forever, I thought to myself. Mitsuko was sitting with her legs stretched out; crouching there in the dusk beside her, I could see her beautiful face in profile, but it was too dark to make out its expression. Beyond the tips of her white tabi socks, silhouetted against the dim twilight sky, there was only the faint glint of the golden dolphins on the roof of the Great Buddha Hall.

"It's late. Let's go back," she said abruptly. By the

time we had walked down the hill to the station, it was around seven o'clock.

"I'm hungry—what about you?" I asked.

Mitsuko seemed worried about the time. "I was supposed to be home early today. I didn't tell anyone I was going to Nara."

"But I'm starved. If it's already so late, what difference would it make?" And I dragged her along to a little steak house.

▼

"Doesn't your husband complain when you're late getting home?" she asked, as we were eating.

"He's used to it," I said. "And I've already told him we're friends."

"What does he think of that?"

"I raved about you so much he even said we should have you over, he'd like to meet you."

"He sounds awfully good-natured."

"The fact is, that husband of mine just lets me do as I please; he never complains. He's so good-natured he's boring. . . ."

Until that moment I hadn't said a word to Mitsuko about myself, but then I told her everything: how I happened to marry, and all the trouble I had over my love affair, and even about how kind *you* were to let me ramble on and on about my problems, in spite of your being so busy.

Mitsuko was astonished to hear I knew you.

"Really, you're a friend of his?" she said, and wondered if I wouldn't bring her with me to meet you someday, since she loved your novels. Whenever I saw her she asked me to take her along next time, but some-how we never got around to it.

Mitsuko was terribly curious to hear about that affair.

"Oh? You aren't seeing him anymore?" she asked, and when I told her I wasn't, she said: "Why not, if it's as romantic as all that? If I were you, I'd make a clear distinction between love and marriage." And then: "Does your husband suspect anything?"

"Possibly, but if he does he's never mentioned it. At least it hasn't caused any trouble between us."

"He's very trusting!"

"Actually, he treats me like a child," I said. "That annoys me."

▼

It was close to ten by the time I got home that night. "Pretty late, aren't you?" my husband said, looking glum.

He seemed so cheerless that I was a little sorry for him. Although I hadn't done anything wrong, I felt a twinge of guilt when I saw that he had just finished dinner, after waiting such a long time for me. Of course when I was meeting my lover, I often used to come home after ten o'clock. But that was all in the past. So maybe he *was* a bit suspicious. Somehow I myself felt just the way I did in those days.

5

OH YES, and that was around the time I finished the Kannon picture and showed it to my husband.

"Hmm, so this is a portrait of your friend Mitsuko? I must say, you've outdone yourself."

We were having dinner, and he had spread the painting out on the tatami mats and would glance at it between one mouthful and the next. "But is she really all that beautiful?" he went on doubtfully. "Are you sure it looks like her?"

"Of course it does, or there wouldn't have been such a fuss over it! Only, the real Mitsuko isn't just an ethereal beauty; there's something sensual about her. You can't bring that out in a Japanese painting."

I had put a great deal of effort into the picture and couldn't help thinking it had turned out well. My husband praised it lavishly. At any rate, from the time I began to study painting I had never worked so hard or with so much enthusiasm.

"Why don't we have it mounted?" he suggested.

"Then when it's ready you can ask Mitsuko over to see it."

The idea appealed to me, and I put it away, thinking I'd take it to a picture mounter in Kyoto to be done up handsomely. One day I mentioned to Mitsuko what I had in mind.

"If you're going to bother to mount it, how about working on it a little more?" she asked. "Of course it's very nice as it is—the face is good—but the figure doesn't seem quite right."

"It doesn't? How is that?"

"I can't tell you in so many words."

She was being perfectly honest; there wasn't the least bit of boastfulness in her tone, the least hint that she thought her own figure was better. But I could see that she felt dissatisfied.

"Well, then, I hope you'll pose in the nude for me sometime."

She agreed at once. "I don't mind posing for you."

▼

I think it was after school one day that she promised to come to pose at my house; the very next afternoon we left classes early and Mitsuko came home with me.

On the way she said: "I'm afraid your husband will be shocked if he sees me standing there naked." She seemed amused rather than embarrassed and glanced at me mischievously as if we were out on a lark.

"We have just the place for it," I told her. "It's a Western-style room upstairs, where no one will see us."

When I took her up to our bedroom, on the second floor, Mitsuko exclaimed: "How absolutely delightful!

And with such a stylish big double bed!" She plumped down on the bed and set the springs rocking as she gazed out at the sea.

Our house is right on the beach, so we have a splendid view from that upstairs room. There are plate-glass windows to the east and south—in the morning it's too bright to let you sleep late. When the weather is clear you can see beyond the pine forests across the bay, all the way to the Kishu Mountains and Mount Kongo.

. . . Swimming? Yes, you can swim there. Along that part of the shore it's dangerous—if you go too far out, the ocean floor drops off suddenly—but there's a bathing beach at Koroen. In the summer it's quite crowded. At that time it was still mid-May, and Mitsuko said: "I wish summer would come soon. I'd be over here every day to swim." Then, looking around the room, she added: "When I'm married I want a bedroom just like this."

"You'll have a much grander bedroom. A girl like you will marry into a rich family, won't you?"

"Yes, but once I'm married I expect I'll feel like a bird in a gilded cage."

"I feel like that myself sometimes. . . ."

"But isn't this a private sanctuary for you and your husband, as a married couple? Won't he scold you for bringing me up here?"

"Why should he object? You're a very special visitor."

"Anyway, people say a couple's bedroom is sacred. . . ."

"Then it's exactly the place to pose—a young girl's

body is sacred too. Hurry up and take your clothes off while the light is good," I urged her.

"Can't someone look in from the ocean?"

"Don't be silly! What could you see from a boat offshore?"

"Yes, but these windows . . . I'd like you to close them and draw the curtains!"

Although it was only May, the sun was so brilliant it hurt your eyes, and all the windows had been thrown open. But with the windows shut tight, the room was soon hot enough to have us dripping with sweat. Mitsuko said she wanted some kind of white cloth to put on as Kannon's robe, so I pulled a sheet from the bed. Then she went behind the wardrobe cabinet, took off her sash and ki-mono, let down her hair, combed it out straight and smooth, and draped the sheet loosely around her naked body in the manner of a Kannon bodhisattva.

"Just look!" she said, standing before the mirror on the door of the cabinet, absorbed in her own beauty. "Now don't you think you've got to touch up your picture?"

"My, what an exquisite body!"

No doubt I seemed to be accusing her, as if I wanted to know why she had concealed such a treasure from me all this time. I suppose the face in my picture was a good likeness, but it's only natural that the figure wasn't, since I had based it on Miss Y. Models for Japanese painting are chosen for their pretty faces, and Miss Y didn't have an especially good figure—her skin, too, seemed rather rough and dark, almost muddy, so that to a trained eye it was as different from Mitsuko's as ink from snow.

"Why have you kept such a beautiful body hidden!" I asked reproachfully. "It's too much! It's just too much!"

Somehow my eyes filled with tears. Embracing Mitsuko from behind, I nestled my tearful face against her white-robed shoulder, and we peered into the mirror together.

Mitsuko seemed disconcerted.

"Really, what has come over you?" she asked, as she saw my tears reflected in the mirror.

"Anything so beautiful makes me want to cry," I said, holding her tight. I didn't try to wipe away my tears.

6

"THERE, THAT OUGHT TO DO," said Mitsuko. "Now I'm getting dressed."

"No, no you mustn't!" I shook my head petulantly. "Let me look at you some more!"

"That's ridiculous. I can't just stay here naked like this, can I?'

"Of course you can! And you're not really naked! You've got to take *this* off—" As I spoke I snatched hold of the sheet that was draped around her, but she struggled to hang on to it, screaming: "Let go! Let go!" Finally I heard the sheet begin to tear.

That drove me into a frenzy, and now my eyes filled with angry tears. "All right then, never mind! I didn't think you were such a coward—this is the end of our friendship!" And I bit a fold of the sheet, sinking my teeth into it and pulling hard, tearing it all the more.

"You must be crazy!"

"I've never known anyone so *cold*! Didn't we

promise not to hide anything from each other? Liar!"

At that moment I'm sure I did seem possessed. As Mitsuko told me later, I was glaring at her, deathly pale and trembling as if I had actually gone mad. And Mitsuko herself trembled as she stared silently into my eyes. She had abandoned the noble pose of the Willow Kannon and was standing there with one knee bent, the tips of her feet touching, her arms crossed shyly before her, looking pathetically beautiful. I felt a stab of pity for her, but when I glimpsed her plump white shoulders through the torn sheet I wanted to rip it off violently. Now I was really frantic and started stripping the sheet from her body. Faced with my determination, Mitsuko seemed to quail. She said nothing and let me do as I pleased. We stared unwaveringly into each other's eyes with an almost hateful intensity. Then a smile at having finally had my way—a cool, malicious smile of triumph—came to my lips as I peeled off the remnants of the sheet. At last the sculptural form of a divine maiden was fully revealed, and my exultation changed to astonishment.

"Ah, how maddening!" I cried, tears flowing down my cheeks. "Such a beautiful body! I could kill you!" As I spoke I grasped her trembling wrist tight with one hand and with the other drew her face near as I brought my lips toward it.

Suddenly I heard Mitsuko cry out wildly. "Go ahead and kill me! I *want* you to!"

I felt her hot breath on my face and saw tears streaming down her own cheeks. Locking our arms around each other, we swallowed our mingled tears.

▼

That day, though without meaning to hide it from him, I'd said nothing to my husband about bringing Mitsuko home with me, and he had waited in his office, thinking I would stop in on my way back from school. As time went on and I still hadn't turned up, he telephoned home. "You might have let me know. I've been waiting all afternoon."

"I'm sorry, it slipped my mind—we came here on an impulse."

"Is Mitsuko still with you?"

"Yes, but I expect she'll be leaving any minute."

"Well, ask her to stay on a little while. I'll be right along."

"Then hurry up, please."

That's what I said, but in my heart I didn't like the thought of his coming home. After what had happened in the bedroom that afternoon, a joyous feeling had welled up within me. What a wonderful day this had been! I was walking on air; the slightest thing was enough to set my heart beating like a drum. I felt that having my husband return would spoil that precious feeling. All I wanted was to be alone with Mitsuko, to go on being together. We needn't even talk; I could simply gaze at her in silence. . . . Just to be there beside her gave me boundless happiness.

"Listen, Mitsuko," I said. "That phone call was from my husband. He says he's coming home. What are you going to do?"

"Oh dear, what *should* I do?"

Mitsuko hastily began putting on her clothes. It was

already five o'clock, two or three hours since she had draped herself in that sheet. "Is it all right for me to leave without seeing him?"

"He's been saying he wants to meet you. . . . Do you mind waiting a little longer?"

Although I asked her to stay, the truth was that I hoped she would leave before he came home. I wanted the whole day to be a happy one; I didn't want its beautiful memory marred by a third person. That was how I felt, so naturally I was out of sorts when my husband arrived. I must have seemed in a bad mood. Even Mitsuko had hardly anything to say, partly because of my attitude, partly because she was meeting him for the first time. Maybe she felt guilty too. All three of us seemed distracted and ill at ease, as if we were preoccupied with our own thoughts. That made me even more irritated at having been disturbed. I was very angry with my husband.

"And how have you girls been amusing yourselves?" he asked, trying to start up a conversation there with Mitsuko.

"Today we used our bedroom as a studio," I put in dryly. "I wanted to improve my Kannon portrait, so I had Mitsuko pose for me."

"That's giving your model a lot of trouble, isn't it, when you're not all that talented to begin with."

"Yes, but I was asked to, for the sake of the model's honor."

"No matter how often you paint her, you can't hope to succeed. Your model is much too pretty."

During that little exchange Mitsuko just giggled, looking down shyly. The conversation died, and she soon left for home.

7

I BROUGHT ALONG some old letters we sent each other in those days, if you care to look at them. There are lots more. I couldn't possibly bring them all, so here are just a few you might find interesting. Please begin with the earliest ones; they're more or less in order. I saved every letter from Mitsuko, and you'll find some of my own among them too—I'll explain later, but there's a reason why she brought them back.

▼

(*Author's note*: the letters that the widow Kakiuchi called "just a few" from their correspondence filled a silk-crepe parcel about ten inches square almost to bursting; the four corners of the cloth had been knotted together with difficulty. Her fingertips crimsoned as she pinched the hard little knot to undo it. What finally came pouring out was a flood of figured paper: all those letters were in envelopes adorned with coquettish, brilliantly colored woodblock designs. The envelopes were small, only big enough to hold a sheet of women's letter paper folded in four, and they were decorated with evening primroses, lilies of the valley, tulips, portraits of beauties in the manner of Takehisa Yumeji, printed in four or five colors. I was somewhat taken aback at the sight. Doubtless no Tokyo woman would choose such garish envelopes. Even for a love letter, she would prefer something plainer. If you showed her such things, you may be certain she would disdain them as hopelessly vulgar. And a man who received a love letter in an envelope like that, supposing he was a Tokyo man, would surely take an instant dislike to the sender. In any case, the taste for that sort of gaudy excess is indeed typical of Osaka women. And when you think that these love letters were exchanged by two women, they seem all the more excessive. Here I will only quote from several of them to illustrate the fervid emotional situation underlying this account, but it may be well to add a description of the stationery itself. In my opinion, the decorative aspect of the letters is sometimes even more revealing than their content.)

▼

(May 6, from Mrs. Kakiuchi Sonoko to Mitsuko. The dimensions of the envelope are 5 inches in length by 2 3/4 inches in width, with cherry and heart-shaped designs on a pink ground. There are five cherries in all, bright-red fruit on black stems. The hearts, of which there are ten, overlap vertically in pairs: those above are pale purple; those below, gold. The notched top and bottom of the envelope is also edged in gold. Ivy leaves printed in very light green cover the surface of the letter paper, over which ruled lines are drawn in silver dots. Mrs. Kakiuchi writes by pen, but the precision of her abbreviated characters shows that she must have had considerable training in calligraphy and no doubt excelled in the subject at school. Her writing suggests a softer version of the calligraphic style of Ono Gado— elegantly flowing, one might say, or, to put it less kindly, somewhat slippery and unctuous. It is singularly well matched to the design of the envelope.)

Dearest Mitsu,

Drip-drop, drip-drop . . . Tonight the gentle spring rain is falling. As I listen to it drenching the paulownia flowers outside my window, I sit here quietly at my desk in the glow of that red lampshade that you crocheted for me. Somehow it's a gloomy evening, but when I strain to hear the raindrops run from the eaves I can't help imagining that they're whispering softly to me: Drip-drop, drip-drop . . . What can they be whispering? Drip-drop, drip-drop . . . Ah, yes! Mitsuko, Mitsuko, Mitsuko . . . They're calling the name of the one I love. Tokumitsu, Toku-mitsu . . . Mitsuko, Mitsuko . . . Toku, Toku, Toku . . . Mitsu, Mitsu, Mitsu . . . Before I knew it, I'd taken up my pen and was writing your name over and over on the fingertips of my left hand, from my thumb to my little finger, one after another. . . .

Forgive me all this foolishness.

Is it odd of me to write letters, when I see you every day? But at school I feel embarrassed to come up to you, I'm strangely self-conscious! To think we

*used to flaunt our intimacy in front of everyone,
before we were like this, but now that the rumors are
true, we seem to be afraid of letting anyone see us!
Does that mean I'm timid after all? Ah, how I wish
I could be strong! Stronger and stronger—strong
enough not to be afraid of the gods, of Buddha, of my
parents, my husband . . .*

*Are you having your tea-ceremony lesson to-
morrow afternoon? Won't you come to my house at
three? Please give me your answer, yes or no, at
school tomorrow, with the usual signal. Do, do come!
Even now the white peony blooming in the azure
vase on my table breathes a tender sigh as she waits
for you, just as I do. If you disappoint her, I'm afraid
the pretty little peony will weep. And the mirror on
the wardrobe cabinet says she wants to reflect your
image. So do come!*

*Tomorrow during the noon recreation period I'll
be standing under the plane tree in the schoolyard.
Don't forget our signal.*

Sonoko

(May II, from Mitsuko to Sonoko. Envelope length, 5 1/2
inches; width, 3 inches. Centered on a ground of dusky
rose, a checkerboard pattern two inches wide is scattered
with four-leaf clovers; below it are two overlapping
playing cards, an ace of hearts and a six of spades. The
checkerboard and the clovers are silver, the heart card
red, the spade black; and the letter paper is a plain dark
brown, the text written on a slant, by pen with white ink,

sloping down to the lower-right-hand corner. The writing is less skillful than Sonoko's and seems to have been rapidly scribbled, but the large, bold characters give an agreeable impression of uninhibited liveliness.)

Ma chère soeur Mlle Jardin,

> *Dearest elder sister, today, Mitsu has been in a bad temper all day long! Plucking the flowers out of the alcove, scolding poor innocent Ume (that's the name of the maid who always waits on her)— whenever Sunday comes around, Mitsu's temper is bad. For a whole day she can't go to see her sister! Why can't she come when that awful Mr. Husband is there?*
>
> *At least I'll make a phone call, I thought, but when I tried just now it seems you were off to Naruo with Mr. Husband to pick wild strawberries!*
>
> *Well, do have fun!*
>
> *It's mean! mean!*
>
> *I can't put up with it! I really can't!*
>
> *Mitsu is crying, all alone.*
>
> *Ah, ah—*
>
> *I'm too bitter to say another word.*
>
> Ta soeur Clair

(*Ta soeur* is of course French for "Your sister," and *Clair,* or "light," comes from the literal meaning of the name Mitsuko. *Ma chère soeur,* "My dear sister," and *Mlle Jardin,* "Miss Garden," similarly refer to Sonoko. The reason for writing "Mlle Jardin" rather than "Mme Jardin" is explained as follows in a postscript.)

I won't call my elder sister "Madame."

*Or "Mrs."—how disgusting! The very thought
of it makes me shudder!*

*But it would be terrible if Mr. Husband heard
about this, wouldn't it?*

Be careful!

Why do you sign your letters Sonoko?

Why don't you say "Your sister"?

(May 18, from Sonoko to Mitsuko. Envelope length,
5 inches; width, 2 7/8 inches. The design is crosswise on
a crimson ground dotted in a silver splash pattern: above
the tips of three large cherry blossom petals appears the
upper half of a maiko dancing girl, seen from the back.
This is an exceptionally rich five-color print of crimson,
purple, black, silver, and blue; and the address is on the
other side, since any writing on the face would be difficult to read. As for the letter itself, a sheet of paper 8 1/2
by 5 1/2 inches bears an almost 10-inch-long design of a
white lily with a curved stem stretching off to the left,
against a shaded border of faint pink, leaving only a
third of the space ruled. Minute, delicate handwriting,
its characters smaller than 8-point type, covers the page.)

*It finally happened, what I've been expecting for some
time . . . it finally exploded.*

*Last night was truly violent. If you'd been there,
Mitsu, how it would have shocked you. My own
husband and I—oh, forgive me for talking about us
that way—that awful husband and I had our worst
quarrel in ages. And not just in ages—in our whole*

married life! We've had our differences before, but never a shouting match like the one last night. To think that a mild, docile man like that can get utterly furious! But I suppose it was natural, now that I think of it. I really did say some terrible things. Why am I so stubborn when I'm with him? And why was I especially strong-minded last night? . . . Not that I feel I was in the wrong. That man himself behaved outrageously, calling me a loose woman, shameless, corrupted by reading trashy novels—and as if that wasn't enough, he accused you of being a home-breaker, of intruding into our bedroom. I could put up with his attacking me, but I couldn't bear to hear him talk about my dear Mitsu.

"If I'm such a loose woman, why did you marry me?" I lashed out at him. "You're no real man—did you marry a woman you despise just so her family would pay for your education? You knew what I was like, didn't you? You're a spineless coward!"

All of a sudden he had grabbed up an ashtray, brandished it threateningly, and dashed it against the wall. But he didn't dare touch me; he just turned pale and stood there glaring.

"Go ahead and hit me—I don't care what you do," I taunted him, but even then he didn't answer back. I haven't spoken to him since.

. . . Now I'd like to tell you more about the quarrel I described in that letter. Maybe I'm repeating myself, but my husband and I were basically incompatible; it seemed to be physiological too. We never enjoyed a happy marital life. According to him, I was too self-centered. It's not that we're incompatible, he said; you just won't make an effort. Even though I'm trying my best, it's impossible, with your attitude. There's no such thing as a perfect marriage. That's how it may look from outside, but do you suppose anybody has no complaints, if you really knew them? I wouldn't be surprised if people envied us too; maybe we *are* happy, compared with most. You've been so spoiled by your sheltered upbringing that you expect too much, you don't know how lucky you are. A person like you would never be satisfied, even if she had an ideal husband.

That's the kind of thing he kept saying, but his worldly-wise, know-it-all manner only provoked me all the more. "I don't think you've ever felt deeply about *anything*," I told him scathingly. "A man like you is simply not human." Maybe he *was* trying to get along with me, but our temperaments clashed. He treated me like a child, as if he was humoring me, and that always got on my nerves. Once I even said: "No wonder you think I'm childish, since you were so brilliant at college, but to me you're a living fossil!"

Did that man have any *passion* in his heart? I asked myself. Did he ever cry or show anger or astonishment, like other people? My husband's cold nature didn't just make me feel miserable and lonely; before long it stimulated a kind of spiteful curiosity in me. And that was what led to my earlier love affair, and to the one with Mitsuko, and to everything that happened afterward.

8

ANYWAY, that earlier affair began right after we were married. I was an innocent young girl, still a little timid and naïve, and I felt guilty toward my husband. But by this time, as my letter shows, I had no such feeling. To tell the truth, I'd gone through so much, all unknown to him, that I myself had become quite worldly and more than a little clever at concealing what I was up to. He was blind to that and kept on treating me like a child. At first I could hardly bear his condescending manner, but when I got annoyed he made fun of me even more, until finally I thought: All right, if I seem childish to you, I'll encourage it, I'll pull the wool over your eyes! I can put on a show of being a horribly spoiled little girl, and fret and coax whenever I want to get my own way. So just go ahead, if it pleases you to consider me a child, I said to myself, but aren't *you* the gullible one? Getting around a man like you is the easiest thing in the world!

Mocking him became more and more enjoyable, and I amazed myself by own own skill at playacting. After even a few words from him I would burst into tears or begin shouting angrily. . . .

I'm sure you know this better than I, since you're a novelist, but our state of mind does seem to change completely, depending on circumstances, doesn't it? Before, I would have felt a pang of regret, and thought: Ah, I shouldn't have done that. But by then I was rebellious enough to ridicule my own faintheartedness, asking myself why I was so weak, how I could be so easily intimidated. . . . And even if it was wrong to be secretly in love with another man, what was so bad about being in love with a woman, someone of my own sex? No matter how close we became, a husband had no right to interfere—that was the kind of argument I used to deceive myself. The truth is, my feeling for Mitsuko was ten times, a hundred times stronger than what I had felt for that other man.

Another reason for my boldness was that from his student days my husband was such a dreadfully fussy, proper person that he had no trouble winning my father's confidence. He was so devoted to "common sense," so incapable of understanding anything the least strange or out of the ordinary, that I was sure he would never question my relations with Mitsuko. He would think we were just friends. That's how it was at first—he had no idea how intimate we were—but as time went on he must have begun to be suspicious. No wonder, since I always used to stop at his office on my way home from school, but lately I'd go back alone, ahead of him. And then, about once every three days, Mitsuko would be sure to come over, and the two of us would spend hours closeted together in that upstairs room. It was only to be expected that he'd find it curious, what with the picture never getting done, although I said I was using her as a model. Of course I occasionally went to Mitsuko's house, after I warned her that he seemed to suspect something.

"We have to be careful, Mitsu," I'd say. "Today I'll come to your place, shall I?"

. . . No, Mitsuko's mother didn't have any qualms about me. She knew it was the city councilman who was behind those rumors at school. And I didn't want to stir up any doubts either, so when I visited them I always tried to ingratiate myself. She became a great admirer of "Mrs. Kakiuchi" and told Mitsuko: "I'm glad you've made such a good friend." As things stood, nothing kept me from telephoning or visiting their house every day . . . but besides her mother there was her maid, Ume, the one mentioned in the letter, and other prying eyes. It wasn't the same as being at my house.

"This won't do after all," Mitsuko declared. "Now that my mother trusts you, it'll be a shame if we spoil it." Then she had a suggestion. "I know! How about the new hot-spring resort at Takarazuka?"

So we went off to Takarazuka. As we were going into one of the private baths there, Mitsuko said: "You're so unfair, Sister! You always want to look at me naked, but you never show yourself to me."

"I'm not being unfair," I protested. "Your skin is so beautiful I'm embarrassed to let you see how much darker mine is. I just hope it won't disgust you."

And in fact when I bared myself completely to her

for the first time, I did feel uncomfortable beside her. Not only was Mitsuko's skin a flawless creamy white; she had a slender, superbly proportioned body. By comparison, my own body suddenly seemed ugly. . . .

"You're beautiful yourself, Sister!" she told me. "We're really no different." Later I came to believe her and thought nothing of it. But that first time I felt myself shrink back.

▼

Well, as you saw in Mitsuko's letter, I went to pick strawberries with my husband one Sunday. Actually, I'd been hoping to go to Takarazuka again, but he wanted to take me out to Naruo, since it was such a fine day. Thinking I'd better humor him for once, I reluctantly agreed. But my heart was still with Mitsuko, and I couldn't enjoy the outing. The more I longed for her, the more my husband's efforts at conversation irritated me, even angered me, to the point that I would hardly reply to him. I spent the whole day moping. Apparently that was when he decided he'd have to do something about the situation. As usual, though, he only looked glum, and since he wasn't the kind of person to show his emotions, I had no idea he was so infuriated with me.

When we came home that evening I learned I'd missed a telephone call, and began fuming at everyone in the house. The next morning Mitsuko's reproachful letter arrived. I called her up immediately and arranged to meet at the Hankyu Umeda station. We went directly to Takarazuka, without even stopping off at school. Every day from then on, for the rest of the week, we

went to Takarazuka. That was when we got our matching kimonos, and had the souvenir photo taken that I
showed you. . . .

Then one afternoon a little past three, while we
were talking together in the bedroom again, almost a
week after the strawberry-picking excursion, our maid,
Kiyo, came rushing upstairs to announce that the master
had just returned.

"Really, at this hour?" I exclaimed, all in a fluster.
"Hurry, Mitsu!" I'm sure we both looked nervous as we
went down to greet him.

Meanwhile, my husband had changed from his suit
into a light serge kimono. He frowned slightly when he
saw us, but then remarked casually: "I had nothing to do
today, so I left the office early. You two seem to be
cutting classes yourself." And he added, to me: "How
about a cup of tea and some cakes, since we have a
guest?"

With that, the three of us settled down to polite talk
as if nothing out of the ordinary had happened. But I
was startled when Mitsuko absent-mindedly called me
"Sister."

"Don't be too intimate," I used to tell her. "It's better
for you to call me Sono, rather than Sister. If you get
into the wrong habit, you'll come out with it before
other people."

Yet whenever I said that, she took offense. "I hate it
when you're so distant! Don't you like to have me think
of you as my big sister? . . . Please, let me call you
Sister—I'll be *very* careful if anyone else is around." But
that day it finally did come out.

▼

After Mitsuko left, there was an awkward silence between my husband and me. And the next evening, as if it had just occurred to him, he suddenly asked: "Isn't there something funny going on? I have a hard time trying to understand your behavior lately."

"What's there to understand?" I shot back. "I'm not aware of anything."

"You're on awfully good terms with that girl Mitsuko," he went on. "What exactly is she to you?"

"I'm very fond of Mitsuko! That's why we're such good friends."

"I know you're fond of her, but what does being fond of her mean?"

"It's just a feeling! It isn't something you can *explain*!" I was purposely defiant, thinking I mustn't let him see any weakness in me.

"Don't be so sensitive," he said. "Can't you just tell me calmly? Being 'fond' has all kinds of meanings—besides, there were those rumors at school. I was only asking because I think it's to your disadvantage if people misunderstand. Suppose talk like that gets around; you'll be the one to blame. You're older, and you're a married woman.... How could you face her parents? And it's not just you—I'd have no excuse myself if people thought I'd condoned your behavior."

What he said cut me to the quick, but I remained stubborn.

"That's enough," I told him. "I don't like your meddling in my choice of friends. You can have any friends you want, and I hope you'll let *me* do as I please! Surely I'm responsible for my own actions."

"Well, if you two were ordinary friends, I certainly wouldn't meddle. But taking off from school nearly every day, doing things behind your husband's back, shutting yourselves up alone together—it just doesn't seem healthy."

"Oh? So that's the way you feel about it. With your nasty imagination, aren't *you* the one that's behaving badly?"

"If I'm at fault, I'll apologize. I only hope it's my imagination. But instead of accusing me, shouldn't you search your own conscience? Are you sure you have nothing to be ashamed of?"

"There you go talking like that again! You know I find Mitsuko attractive—that's why we became friends. Didn't you yourself say you wanted to meet her, if she's so beautiful? It's natural to be attracted to beautiful people, and between women it's like enjoying a work of art. If you think that's unhealthy, you're the unhealthy one!"

"All right, but you could enjoy a work of art in front of me; you needn't shut yourselves up together . . . and why do you both look so nervous when I come home? Another thing: it bothers me to hear her call you Sister, when you're not even related."

"Don't be absurd! You haven't the faintest idea of schoolgirl talk, have you? Girls often think of each other as older sister and younger sister, if they're good friends. You're the only one who finds it strange!"

That evening my husband was oddly persistent.

Usually as soon as I seemed irritated he would give up and say: "You're impossible." But this time he kept after me.

"Don't try to lie your way out of it: I've already heard all about it from Kiyo." And he added that he knew I wasn't just painting—he wanted me to confess what I *was* up to.

"There's nothing to confess. I'm not a professional painter hiring a model—it's a diversion for me. I don't have to be so serious and businesslike."

"Then why not work down here, instead of always staying upstairs?"

"What's wrong with working up there? Go and visit an artist in his studio—even a professional isn't always grimly slaving away. You can't make a good painting unless you take your time and work when the spirit moves you."

"That's all very fine, but I wonder if you ever intend to finish it."

"I'm in no hurry. Mitsuko's so beautiful I can't take my eyes off her—not just her face but that lovely body. When she poses for me I could study her hour after hour, even without painting a stroke."

"She doesn't mind if you spend all that time looking at her undressed?"

"Of course not. No woman is embarrassed to show herself to another woman, and no one minds being admired."

"Even so, people would think you were crazy, having a young girl stand around naked in broad daylight."

"That's because I'm not like you, so *conventional*. Didn't you ever want to see a gorgeous movie actress in the nude? To me, it's the same as looking at a beautiful landscape. I'm spellbound; somehow it makes me happy, glad to be alive. Tears come into my eyes. But I suppose you can't explain that to a person who has no sense of beauty."

"What does a sense of beauty have to do with it? You're just being perverse!"

"And you're just narrow-minded."

"Don't be ridiculous! You've poisoned yourself reading sentimental trash."

"And you're insufferable!" I turned away, trying to cut off the argument.

"As for that Mitsuko, I can't believe she's a decent young woman, or she'd never dream of intruding into our bedroom, trying to break up our marriage. She must have an evil character. You'll get into trouble yourself if you keep on seeing somebody like that."

An attack on the one I loved stung far worse than an attack on me, and the moment he started criticizing Mitsuko I flew into a rage. "The very idea! What right have you to say that about my dearest friend? I'm sure there's no one in the whole world as virtuous and beautiful as Mitsuko! She's simply divine—she's as pure in heart as Kannon herself! It's evil of *you* to slander her. You'll be sorry for it!"

"There, you see! You're out of your mind, talking like that! You're a raving lunatic!"

"And you're a living fossil!"

"Somehow you've turned into a terrible, loose woman. You're completely shameless!"

"Isn't that just my own character? Why did you marry a woman like that, when you knew it all along? I suppose you wanted my father to pay for your education and a trip abroad. That must have been the reason."

Even my usually mild-mannered husband was aroused. The veins stood out on his forehead, and for once he roared at me.

"What? Say that again!"

"Yes, I'll say it over and over! You're no real man; you only married me for money. Spineless coward!"

Then suddenly he drew himself up and shook his fist at me, and something white came whizzing by and crashed against the wall. I ducked instinctively, so I wasn't touched, but he had picked up an ashtray and thrown it. Never before had he raised a hand against me, and my temper flared.

"Is *that* how you feel? I'm warning you—if I get the slightest scratch, my father will know about it. So go ahead and do your worst. Beat me! Kill me! I want you to! I told you to kill me!"

"Idiot!"

That was all he said. He looked at me in disbelief as I yelled at him, weeping and half-crazed.

Neither of us said another word. The next day we only glared at each other, keeping silent even after we went to our bedroom that evening. But around midnight my husband turned to me and grasped my shoulder, drawing me toward him. I pretended to be asleep and let him do it.

"I went a little too far myself last night," he said. "Still, you must realize it's because I love you. I may seem cold, with my blunt manner, but I don't think my heart is cold. If I'm at fault I'll try to correct it—can't you respect the one thing I ask? I won't interfere with you in anything else, only please stop seeing Mitsuko. Just promise me that much."

"No!" I shook my head vigorously, my eyes still closed.

"If you won't, you won't, but at least don't bring her into this room or go anywhere alone with her. And from now on let's go out and come back together too."

"No!" I shook my head again. "I can't stand being tied down—I've got to be absolutely free!"

With that, I turned my back to him.

9

AFTER THAT OUTBURST I wasn't afraid of anything. Why should I care? I longed all the more to be with Mitsuko. But when I hurried to school the next morning she was nowhere in sight. I called her home, only to be told she had gone to visit a relative in Kyoto. Eager to see her, and with the emotions of last night's quarrel surging in me, I dashed off that letter, but after I sent it I asked myself what she would think of a frantic letter like that. Suddenly I felt anxious again, wondering if she might say she felt guilty toward my husband and had better keep her distance.

Then the following morning, as I was waiting in the shade of the plane tree, she came running up to me, calling out "Sister!" in front of everyone.

"I just got your letter, Sister, and I was so worried I couldn't wait to see you!"

Putting her arms around my shoulders, she gazed up at me, tears in her eyes.

"Oh dear, Mitsu, you must be upset by what my husband said about you. . . ." I began to cry too. "Does it make you angry? I'm sorry; I shouldn't have written that letter."

"It's not that—as long as it's just about me, I don't care what anyone says. But are you sure he hasn't turned *you* against me? Are you quite sure, Sister?"

"Silly! Would I have written to you that way, or tried to phone you? How could I bear to part from you, whatever happens? If he grumbles about it, he'll be the one to pay!"

"That's what you think now, Sister, but I wonder if you won't get tired of me. Maybe it's your husband you love after all. They say married couples are like that. . . ."

"I don't consider myself married to that man. I'm still my own woman. If you're willing to run away together, Mitsu, I'll run away with you—anywhere you like!"

"Oh, Sister! You will? Are you sure of that?"

"Of course I am! I'm ready to leave anytime."

"I'm ready too! And what if I said I was going to die: would you die with me, Sister?"

"Yes, yes, I'd die with you! Would you really die with me, Mitsu?"

▼

And so our relationship deepened after that quarrel with my husband. Still, he said nothing, perhaps because he had given up. I took advantage of that to become even bolder.

"He's resigned to it," I told Mitsuko. "There's nothing to worry about."

So she became bolder too, and if he came home while we were in the bedroom, she would tell me not to go down to greet him. Of course she wouldn't go downstairs herself. Sometimes she stayed until ten or eleven o'clock at night.

"Sister, could you please phone home for me?" she'd ask, and I'd assure her mother she was having dinner with us and would be ready to leave at such and such an hour. Then her maid, Ume, would come after her in a taxi. Often we had dinner alone upstairs, but sometimes I invited my husband to join us since he had nothing else to do; he always agreed, and the three of us would eat together. By now Mitsuko never hesitated to call me Sister in his presence. When she wanted to talk to me, she would phone me even in the middle of the night.

"What is it, Mitsuko, at this hour? You're still awake?"

"Did you go to bed already, Sister?"

"But it's past two o'clock. . . . I was sound asleep."

"Well, *do* forgive me . . . just when you were enjoying your nice warm bed together."

"Mitsu, is that why you called me?"

"It's all very well for somebody with a husband, but I'm here all by myself, and I feel *lonely*. As late as it is, I just can't sleep."

"Really, you're hopeless! Stop fretting and go to bed! You can come to see me tomorrow."

"I'll come as soon as I'm awake, so be sure to get that husband of yours out of bed early!"

"All right, don't worry."

"You're sure, now?"

"Yes, I understand."

We would spend twenty or thirty minutes on the telephone talking nonsense like that. Gradually our secret notes and letters were not so secret either, and I would leave a letter from Mitsuko lying open on the desk. . . . Of course my husband was not the sort to read other people's mail on the sly, I needn't worry about that, but in the past, once I'd read a letter, I used to hurry to lock it away in a cabinet drawer. . . .

▼

As things were going, I realized I might be in for another stormy session with my husband at any moment, but we were getting along better just then, so I let myself become more and more infatuated, a slave to passion, and in the midst of it came something I hadn't dreamed of—an absolute bolt from the blue. That was on the third of June. Mitsuko had come over around noon and stayed until about five P.M., after which my husband and I finished dinner together at eight o'clock; about an hour later, a little past nine, the maid told me I had a phone call from Osaka. "From Osaka? Who could that be?"

"They didn't say," Kiyo replied. "They wanted you to come to the phone right away."

When I went to the telephone and asked who was calling, all I heard was: "It's me—it's me, Sister." That sounded as if it had to be Mitsuko. But I could hardly make out the words, whether because the connection was bad or the other person was talking in such a low voice, and I felt that someone might be playing a trick on me.

"Who is this?" I insisted. "Please speak up and give me your name. What number are you calling?"

"It's *me*, Sister. I'm calling Nishinomiya 1234." The moment I heard that voice repeat our telephone number, I knew it had to be Mitsuko. "Listen, I'm in Osaka, down by Namba, and something terrible has happened—I've had my clothes stolen!"

"Your *clothes*? . . . What on earth were you doing?"

"I was taking a bath. It's a restaurant in the pleasure quarter, so they have a Japanese bath—"

"But why would you be in a place like that?"

"Well, actually, I've been wanting to tell you about it, Sister—anyway, you can hear all that later. . . . I'm in a terrible fix—please help me. I need that matching kimono of yours, just as soon as I can!"

"So you went straight to Osaka after you left here?"

"Mm, yes."

"Who's there with you?"

"Somebody you wouldn't know, Sister. . . . If I don't get that kimono, I can't go home tonight. *Please*, I'm begging you, won't you have someone bring it to me?"

Mitsuko's voice sounded tearful. For my part, I was so disturbed that my heart was pounding and my knees had begun to tremble. But I asked where to take it, and she told me she was at a place called the Izutsu, a restaurant I'd never heard of, in Kasayamachi, on a pleasure quarter street south off the Tazaemon Bridge avenue. In addition to the kimono, she wanted a certain matching sash and its fastenings, which luckily I also had, along with a waistband and inner sash and socks. It seemed strange that all those things had been stolen too.

"What about the underslip?" I asked.

"No," she said. "They spared me that much."

I was to have a trustworthy person deliver everything within the hour, by ten o'clock at the latest, so I decided I couldn't leave it to anyone else: I had no choice but to hurry there in a taxi myself.

When I asked if it was all right for me to bring the clothes, I thought I heard someone beside her at the phone coaching her on what to say.

"Maybe that *would* be better, Sister . . . or you could give them to Ume; she must be waiting for me at the Hanshin station in Umeda by now. She doesn't know where I am, so you'll have to tell her how to come. And have her ask for Suzuki."

Then I heard another whispered consultation. After a while Mitsuko went on, hesitantly: "And, Sister . . . I'm really sorry to bother you, but somebody else lost his clothing. Could you possibly bring along one of your husband's kimonos, or a suit? It doesn't matter which." And then: "One more thing . . . I'd be ever so grateful if you could bring twenty or thirty yen too."

"I can manage that," I said. "Just wait for me."

After I hung up, I immediately called a taxi. All I told my husband was that I'd be going in to Osaka briefly—Mitsuko needed some help. Then I went upstairs to the cabinet and hastily took out my matching kimono and the accessories, along with one of my husband's best summer kimonos of silk serge, a tie-dyed sash, and a haori coat. I wrapped all of it together in a cloth parcel and had the maid spirit it out to the entrance hall for me.

Sure enough, he seemed suspicious. "Why are you taking her a parcel at this hour?" he asked, coming out of the house just as I was ready to get into the taxi. Probably I looked flustered and pale; of course it *was* odd for me to be going somewhere without changing clothes or tidying my hair.

"I don't know why, but she wants my matching kimono," I said, deliberately pulling an edge of it past the knot of the parcel to show him. "She has to have it, she says, and I'm to take it to their shop in Osaka. Maybe she's going to be in some kind of amateur theatrical. Anyway, I'll ask the taxi to wait, and come right back."

▼

At first I thought I'd go directly to that Izutsu restaurant, since it was already so late—it must have been about nine-thirty—but then I decided I'd better go to the Hanshin station and pick up Ume, to try to find out how much she knew. When I reached the station I saw her standing by the central entrance, looking around impatiently. I called to her and beckoned from the taxi.

"Oh, it's you, Mrs. Kakiuchi!" She seemed embarrassed as well as startled.

"You're waiting for Mitsu, aren't you?" I said. "Something awful has happened; she phoned me to come right away. You come too!"

"My, is that so?"

Ume hesitated, as if she didn't know what to think, but I drew her into the taxi and gave her the gist of our telephone conversation as we went along.

"Who could that be, the man with her? Can you tell me, Ume?" She was tongue-tied at first and looked very distressed, but I kept after her. "Surely you know something about it. This isn't the only time she's been out with him, is it? I won't cause you any trouble, whatever comes of this, and you'll be well rewarded. . . ." I let her see me take out a ten-yen note and fold a sheet of paper around it.

"No, no," she protested, "you're too kind."

But I slipped it into her sash. "Let's not waste any more time."

"I wonder if I ought to go along with you, Mrs. Kakiuchi, to a place like that. Won't I get scolded?"

"Why should you? She wanted me to have you come, if I couldn't."

"Did she tell you all that on the phone? It makes me nervous. . . ."

Ume seemed to feel I was luring her into a trap. "There's nothing to be afraid of," I said, to reassure her. "I only know about it because Mitsu called me."

"Yes, but I've wondered why you didn't notice anything before. That's been bothering me all along. . . ."

"Oh? And how long *has* it been going on?"

"A long time—at least since April; I'm not really sure."

"Who is this man she's with?"

"I don't know that either. She gives me money and tells me to go to a movie, and then wait for her at Umeda at a certain time. I can't imagine where she goes. I thought she might have been meeting you somewhere. Even when we get home late, she wants me to say we were at Mrs. Kakiuchi's house."

10

I ASKED UME how often it had happened

"That's hard to say too. She'd tell me she was going to her tea-ceremony lesson, or to Mrs. Kakiuchi's . . . but she'd always seemed agitated. Now I have to do an errand, she'd say, and go off alone."

"Are you sure you're telling me the truth?"

"Why would I lie to you? Didn't you suspect it yourself, Mrs. Kakiuchi? Didn't you ever think something was going on?"

"I'm just too stupid. All this time I've been treated badly, simply walked all over, and I never knew it till this very day. What cruel behavior?"

"Yes, I'm afraid my young mistress doesn't have much of a conscience. . . . Whenever I see you, I feel guilty. I'm so sorry for you. . . ."

Ume seemed genuinely sympathetic, and much as I disliked confiding in her, I had become so bitter, so distraught, that I wanted to tell her everything that was on my mind.

"Listen, Ume, you must have known how I felt. I never dreamed of anything like this. Lately I've been quarreling terribly with my husband over Mitsu. If I hadn't been so wrapped up in her I'd surely have caught on, no matter how dull-witted I seem. Well, never mind, but how on earth could she telephone me like that tonight? She must take me for a fool!"

"Really, how *could* she! But maybe she was at her wits' end."

"I don't care what trouble she was in—how could she dare to tell me she went to a restaurant with her boyfriend and they had a bath there! You can draw your own conclusions!"

"Yes, of course, but still, once she had her clothes stolen she couldn't go home naked. . . .'"

"I'd have done it. Rather than make such a shameless phone call, I'd have gone home stark naked!"

"And to get robbed at a time like that—it doesn't pay to keep bad company."

"Anyway, it serves them right—not just to lose their money but to lose all their clothes, right down to their underwear. . . ."

"Yes, yes indeed. It serves them right!"

"When we got our matching kimonos, it wasn't for a thing like this. . . . How far will she go to take advantage of me?"

"It was awfully lucky my mistress wore that kimono today! What could she have done if you hadn't worried about her, Mrs. Kakiuchi? What if you told her you wouldn't come: she'd have to get out of it the best way she knew how."

"I thought about doing just that. But at first I couldn't imagine *what* was going on, I was so startled by that tearful voice over the phone. And hateful as she was, I couldn't bring myself to hate her, so when I suddenly pictured her there, naked and trembling, I felt a rush of pity. . . . That may seem ridiculous to you, Ume, looking at it from outside, but that's exactly how it was."

"Oh yes, I can see what you must have felt. . . ."

"And then asking me to bring the man's things too, not just things for herself, and whispering together right at the telephone, as if they wanted me to hear—how could she! She used to call me Sister in front of everyone, and said she's never let anyone but me see her in the nude—I wonder how they looked, naked there together!"

▼

By then I was talking so wildly I hardly knew where we were. Apparently we had turned west off Sakai Avenue at Shimizucho; I remember seeing the lights of the Daimaru department store on Shinsaibashi beyond us, but before we got to it we headed south along the Tazaemon Bridge avenue, and the taxi driver said: "This is Kasayamachi—where do you want to get off?"

"I'm looking for a restaurant called the Izutsu," I said.

We drove around for a while but couldn't find it, and when we asked someone in the neighborhood, we were told it wasn't a restaurant at all, it was really an inn.

"And where is that?" I inquired.

"Down the little side street just ahead."

Even though it wasn't far from Soemoncho and Shinsaibashi Avenue, the whole area was dark and rather lonely. There were a number of geisha houses and little restaurants and inns, but they were all narrow, modest buildings, as quiet as private houses. From the entrance to the side street that had been pointed out to us, we could see hanging from one of the eaves a lamp with the words "Hotel Izutsu" in small characters.

"Wait here for me, Ume," I said, and went on alone.

Although it called itself a hotel, the Izutsu was a dubious-looking establishment at the end of the street. I hesitated a moment after opening its lattice door, but someone seemed to be busy on the telephone in the kitchen, and I called out over and over, with no response. Finally I shouted a loud "Hello!" and a maid came out. As soon as she saw me she seemed to know who I was. Before I could say another word, she asked me to come in and led me up a stairway to the second floor.

"Here's the lady you were expecting," she announced, opening a sliding door. I went into a little three-mat antechamber and found a fair-skinned young man in his twenties sitting there on the floor in a formal posture.

"Excuse me, but are you the lady who is a friend of Mitsuko's?" he asked.

When I said I was, he stiffened and then made a deep bow, all the way down to the floor.

"I don't know how to apologize for what happened tonight," he said. "Mitsuko will have to give you her own explanation shortly. She says she can't bear to face you, especially the way she looks now, so please wait until she has had time to put on the kimono you were good enough to bring her."

The young man had the sort of regular features and feminine good looks that were likely to appeal to Mitsuko; his slender eyebrows and narrow eyes gave an impression of slyness, but the moment I saw him I thought: What a handsome boy! He was supposed to have lost his clothes too, but he was wearing a neat unlined kimono of ordinary striped silk—later I heard he had borrowed it from one of the hotel employees.

"Here's the change of clothing I brought you," I said, handing him the package.

He accepted it politely. "Thank you very much," he said, and he opened a sliding door in the corner, thrust the package into the inner room, and quickly shut the door again, so that I had only a glimpse of a low bed screen. . . .

▼

It would take an awfully long time to tell you everything that happened that night. Anyway, I had delivered the clothing I brought for them, and since he was there, I decided it was useless to see Mitsuko. So I wrapped the thirty yen in paper and told him: "I'll leave now—please give this to Mitsuko."

He wouldn't hear of my going.

"No, no, please stay—she'll be right out," he said, and settled himself down before me once again. "Actually, this is something Mitsuko herself will have to explain, but I think I owe you an explanation of my own. I hope you'll be willing to listen to what I have to say."

Obviously Mitsuko found it hard to talk to me, and they had arranged to have him speak for her while she was changing clothes. And then this suave fellow—oh, at that point he said: "My wallet was taken, so I don't have a calling card, but my name is Watanuki Eijiro. I live near Mr. Tokumitsu's shop in Semba." What this Watanuki told me was that while Mitsuko was still living in Semba, around the end of last year, he and Mitsuko had fallen in love and had even intended to be married. However, this spring the talk of marriage with M had come up, and they were afraid their own plans were doomed. Fortunately the rumor of a lesbian affair had the effect of breaking off M's proposal.

. . . Well, that was more or less how he began. They never tried to use me, he insisted, even if it might have seemed that way at first. But gradually Mitsuko had been stirred by my own passion and had fervently returned my love, more than she ever loved him. He felt unbearably jealous; if anyone was used, it was he himself. And although he had never met me before, he had heard all about me from Mitsuko. She told him that love between women was entirely different from their kind of love, and if he wouldn't let her see me she wouldn't go on seeing him either. Lately he had yielded to her wish.

"My sister has a husband too," Mitsuko would say, "and I'm willing to marry you. But married love is one thing and love for another woman is something else, so please realize that I won't give up Sister as long as I live. If you can't accept that, I won't marry you."

Mitsuko's feeling for me was absolutely sincere, Watanuki said. Again I felt I was being made a fool of, but he was really a smooth-talking fellow and didn't leave any room for me to argue with him. It was wrong to go on hiding his relations with Mitsuko from me, he thought, and he had told her to ask me to agree to the situation, since he had already agreed. Mitsuko understood that it was clearly for the best, but whenever we were face-to-face she found it hard to come out with. She kept thinking there might be a better opportunity, until finally things had turned out as they did tonight.

Also, Mitsuko had said over the phone that they were robbed, but in fact it wasn't an ordinary robbery—the people who had taken their clothes weren't robbers; they were gamblers. The more he told me, the truer it seemed that a bad deed never goes unpunished. That night some people were gambling in another room at the inn, he said, and it seems there was a police raid. When Mitsuko and he heard all the commotion, they were so alarmed they fled blindly from their room, she in her underslip and he himself in his nightclothes, escaping by the roof over to the next-door house, where they hid under the floor of a laundry drying platform. The gamblers took off in all directions: Most of them got away, but one laggard couple came wandering in confusion down the corridor past the open door to their room, just after the two of them had left, and went in to hide. Then this man and woman decided to pretend they were there on a rendezvous—it seems they understood that the detectives in charge of rounding up gamblers were different from the ones who were after illicit lovers. But the detectives were too clever for them and arrested them on suspicion, to take them off to the police station. That's when they put on the kimonos that Mitsuko and Watanuki had left in the clothes box by their bedside.

You see, this couple had changed into inn robes to gamble, and during the raid their own clothes were in a different room. So to keep up the pretense that they weren't gamblers, they had to put on the clothes they found there by the bed. Then when Mitsuko and he at last felt safe enough to come back after their narrow escape, their clothes were gone—they hadn't even been left a wallet or handbag, and the innkeeper had been arrested too, so there was no one to help them. They couldn't even go home.

Another worry, according to Watanuki, was that they might be identified by Mitsuko's Hankyu train pass, which was in her bag, and by the calling cards in his own wallet. It would be disastrous for them if the police carried the investigation to their families; that's why they were at such a loss when she telephoned me. But since I had been kind enough to come all the way here, and seemed to care so much for Mitsuko, perhaps I would also take the trouble to go back with her to Ashiya and say that we had spent the evening together at the movies. And just in case the police had called, he said, he counted on me to find some plausible way to explain it.

11

"PLEASE, MRS. KAKIUCHI, I'm sure you must be angry about tonight, but it's something I have to beg of you." Again he bowed deeply, till his forehead touched the floor. "I don't care what happens to me, but please, please take Mitsuko safely home. I'll be forever grateful." By the end he was clasping his hands prayerfully.

For my part, even though I felt I had been terribly mistreated, I'm so easily moved that I couldn't bring myself to refuse. Still, out of sheer bitterness, I simply glared at him in silence for a time as he groveled there before me. At last I gave in and said merely: "All right."

Watanuki bowed again.

"Aah!" he sighed theatrically, in a voice full of emotion. "So you *will* do it. I'm truly thankful to you; that takes a burden off my mind." Then, peering into my eyes as if to see how I might react, he added: "In that case, I'll ask Mitsuko to come in here, but before I do I have one more request to make. She's so upset by all that's gone on tonight that I hope you won't say anything about it. Is that agreeable? Will you promise not to mention it?"

I couldn't refuse that either, and he immediately called to Mitsuko through the sliding door.

"She understands everything," he assured her. "Please come out!"

A little while before, I had heard a rustling sound beyond the door as she seemed to be putting on the kimono, but by now it was deadly silent, as if she was straining to hear what we were saying. A few minutes after he called to her, the door finally began to open. Little by little, an inch or two at a time, the door slid open, and then Mitsuko appeared, her eyes reddened and swollen from crying.

I wanted to see her expression, but the moment our eyes met she dropped her gaze and slipped quietly down to sit nestled in the young man's shadow. I only saw her bite her lip—saw those swollen eyelids, the long lashes, the elegant line of her nose—as she sat with both hands tucked into her sleeves, leaning in a kind of abandoned pose, her body twisted, the skirt of her kimono gaping in disarray. And as I looked at Mitsuko sitting there, I was reminded that this very kimono was one of our matching pair, and I thought of the time we ordered them and of how we put them on to have our picture taken together. My anger flared up again: Oh, I should never have had that kimono made! I wanted to fly at her and rip it to shreds—really, if we had been alone I might have done just that!

Watanuki seemed to sense this, and before we could say a word he urged us to get ready to leave and went to change clothes himself. Afterward, in spite of the protests of the hotel staff, he insisted on giving them some of the money I'd brought, to settle the bill. And, intent on avoiding the least risk, he had another request for me:

"Oh, yes, Mrs. Kakiuchi . . . I'm sorry to trouble you, but I think it would be best if you made a phone call now to your own house, and to Mitsuko's too."

I'd been worried about things at home myself, so I telephoned our maid and asked her: "Have you heard anything from Mitsuko's family? I'm just about to take her back, and then I'll come home."

"Yes," she replied, "there was a phone call a little while ago, but I didn't know what to tell them. So I didn't say anything about the time, just that you both went in to Osaka."

"Has my husband gone to bed?"

"No, he's still up."

"Tell him I'll be home soon," I said.

Then I called Mitsuko's house. "We went to the movies at the Shochiku tonight," I told her mother when she came to the phone, "and after that we were so hungry we dropped in at the Tsuruya restaurant. It's getting awfully late; I'll bring Mitsuko back right away."

Mitsuko's mother only said: "Oh, is that what happened? It's so late that I telephoned your house." From the way she spoke, it was clear she hadn't heard anything from the police.

▼

Things seemed to be turning out well, and we decided to leave by taxi as soon as possible. The young man had only about half of the thirty yen left, but he began passing out tips to the inn servants to make sure there would be no further trouble, telling them just what to say in case of any investigation by the authorities. Even at such a time he seemed incredibly thorough. Finally we left—I had arrived a little after ten and had spent about an hour there, so it must have been past eleven. Then I remembered I'd had Ume wait for me, and I went out and called to her—she was walking up and down the little street—and had her get in the taxi. Watanuki calmly climbed in too, declaring: "I'll come along part of the way."

Mitsuko and I were side by side in the back seat, and Ume and Watanuki perched on the little folding seats facing us. All four of us sat there across from each other without a word as the taxi sped along. When we came to the Muko Bridge, Watanuki at last broke the silence.

"What do you want to do?" he said, as if the thought had just occurred to him. "I wonder if you shouldn't be coming home on the train.... How about it, Mitsuko?" he asked. "How far do you want to go by taxi?"

That was because Mitsuko lived only five or six hundred yards from the Ashiyagawa station, in the hills west of the river, near the famous Shiomizakura cherry grove. Still, it was a fearfully dangerous road through a lonely pinewoods where there'd been many rapes and robberies; when Mitsuko came home at night, even along with Ume, she always took a taxi from the station. I suggested changing taxis at Ashiyagawa, but Ume said that would never do, the local drivers knew them, so we ought to get another taxi before that.

All this time Mitsuko kept silent. Occasionally she

gave a little sigh and fixed her gaze on Watanuki, across from her, as if telling him something in secret. He looked back at her the same way and said: "Well, maybe we ought to leave this taxi at Narihira Bridge."

I knew very well why he was proposing that. The path to the Hankyu station from the bridge was dangerous too, along an embankment with a row of huge pines, not the sort of place for three women to walk alone. Watanuki simply wanted to be with Mitsuko as long as possible, so he thought of getting out of the taxi and seeing us to the station to find another one. The fact that he knew the bridge and the way to the train, even though he'd said he lived near the Tokumitsu shop in Semba, must have been because they had walked there together often. It made me want to tell him: We can't let anyone see us with a man! If it's just the three of us, we can make some excuse—you ought to go on home. You said *I* should see her to her house, so if you're not leaving, I'll leave myself.

But Ume chimed in, agreeing with everything he proposed. "That's a good idea! Let's do that!" She seemed to be playing into his hands. "It's a lot of trouble for you, but you wouldn't mind coming with us as far as the Hankyu station?"

I began to think Ume was in on the plot. When we left the taxi at the bridge and headed down the pitch-black path along the embankment, she said: "It'd be scary to walk here in the dark without a man along, wouldn't it, Mrs. Kakiuchi?" And she made a point of buttonholing me and telling me how this or that young girl had recently been attacked along this path; meanwhile she saw to it that we kept well ahead of Watanuki and Mitsuko. They were a dozen yards or so behind us, still talking about something—I could barely hear Mitsuko's replies, but she seemed to be agreeing with him too.

Watanuki left us in front of the station, and we three lapsed into silence again as we went by taxi from there to Mitsuko's house.

"My, my!" her mother exclaimed, coming out to meet us. "Why did you ever let it get so late?" She seemed awfully apologetic toward me and thanked me profusely. "I'm sorry we're always causing you so much trouble."

Both Mitsuko and I looked uneasy, afraid we might betray ourselves if the talk went on too long, so when her mother offered to call a taxi for me, I told her I'd had ours wait—and almost fled from the house.

▼

I took the Hankyu back to Shukugawa again and went from there to Koroen by taxi, arriving home just at midnight. Kiyo came to greet me at the door.

"Has my husband gone to bed yet?" I asked.

"He was up till a little while ago," she replied, "but now he's in bed."

That's good, I thought. Maybe he's gone to sleep without knowing I'm back. I opened the bedroom door as quietly as I could and tiptoed in. There was an open bottle of white wine on the bedside table, and my husband seemed to be sleeping peacefully, with the blanket drawn up over his head. Since he was a poor drinker and hardly ever took a drink at bedtime, I supposed he must have had some wine because he was too worried to sleep.

I crept stealthily into bed beside him, trying not to disturb his quiet breathing, but couldn't go to sleep myself. The more I brooded over what had happened, the more bitter and angry I became, until my heart seemed lacerated by rage. How can I manage to avenge myself? I thought. No matter what, I'll make her suffer for it! By then I was so agitated that I found myself reaching out to the table for a half-full glass of wine, and I drank it down in one gulp. Anyhow, I wasn't used to drinking either, and I was so worn out from that hectic evening that the wine went right to my head. It wasn't a pleasant feeling—suddenly I had a splitting headache, as if all the blood in my body had rushed there, and I felt nauseous in the pit of my stomach. Gasping for breath, I was on the verge of crying out: How *dare* you all try to make such a fool of me! Just wait and see! But even as that thought obsessed me, I realized that my heart was beating wildly, like the throb of sake being poured from a cask; soon I noticed that my husband's heart was throbbing the same way and that his hot breath was coming out in gasps too. Our breathing and our palpitations grew more and more violent, in the same rhythm, till it seemed that both our hearts were about to burst, when all at once I felt my husband's arms tight around me. The next moment his panting breath was even nearer and his burning lips grazed my earlobe: "I'm glad you're home!"

Somehow that made tears well up in my eyes, and I burst out: "I've been so humiliated!" Then, racked with sobbing, I turned and clung to him, repeating "Humiliated! Humiliated!" over and over, and I rocked his body fiercely in my arms.

"What is it?" he asked gently. "Who humiliated you? Please, tell me what's wrong—I can't understand you if you're crying, can I? What happened?"

As he spoke, he stroked my tears away, soothing and calming me, but that only made me even more wretched. I was overwhelmed by remorse. Ah, how good he is! I thought. I deserved my punishment. . . . I'll cling to his love from now on, all the rest of my life, and have nothing more to do with her.

"I'll tell you about tonight," I said, "but please do forgive me."

In the end, I told my husband everything.

12

I FELT I HAD had a complete change of heart. The next morning I got up two hours earlier than my husband and went out to the kitchen to prepare his breakfast, after which I carefully laid out his clothes. . . . All those tasks that I'd been in the habit of leaving to the maid I now bustled about taking care of myself.

"Aren't you going to school today?" he asked, while he was tying his necktie at the mirror before leaving for the office.

"I don't think I'll go there anymore," I said, as I stood behind him helping him into his coat. Then I sat down and began folding up the kimono he had just taken off.

"Why not? There's no reason to stop entirely, is there?"

"It's no use going to a school like that . . . and I'd hate to come across somebody I don't want to see again either."

"Hmm. Well, in that case, maybe you ought to stop." My husband seemed grateful but also a little anxious, as if he felt sorry for me. "That isn't the only school around, you know," he went on sympathetically. "If you want to study painting, why not look for a real art school? I like going to the city together in the mornings too."

But I refused. "From now on, I don't want to leave the house. I'm sure I wouldn't get anything out of it, wherever I went."

Beginning that very day, I stayed home working hard from morning till night, determined to be a model housewife. As for my husband's feelings, he seemed delighted by the change in me. Willful as I had been, now I was like a new person. And yet he clearly wanted to return to our old life of going happily back and forth to Osaka together. I, too, wanted to be with him all the time. Apart, I might be subject to wicked fantasies, I thought, but as long as I could see him there beside me, I'd be able to forget Mitsuko. . . . But no, much as I wanted to go out with him, what if I happened to come across her in the street? If I did, I was sure I wouldn't say a word to her, but still, what *would* I do if we suddenly came face-to-face? I'd go pale, and tremble, and be rooted to the spot. I might faint, even at my own doorstep.

So I was afraid to go outside, let alone to Osaka, and one day when I ventured as far as the streetcar line, the mere sight of someone who reminded me of her made me flee back to the house, as if I'd come under a surprise attack. Trying to calm my pounding heart, I told myself: This will never do, I must never go out. For the time being I'll shut myself up at home like a person dead to the world and throw myself into housework—washing, dusting, anything. Every day the thought came to me that I ought to burn those letters stored in the cabinet drawer. Above all, I had to get rid of that Kannon portrait. But whenever I came to the cabinet—Today I'll burn up every scrap! I said to myself—it occurred to me that if I had the letters in my hand I'd surely want to read them. In the end, I was afraid to open the drawer. That was how it went all day long, and when my husband came home in the evening I thought how glad I was and felt that a weight had been taken off my shoulders.

"Nowadays I think about you from morning till night—you're always in my mind. You feel the same way about me, don't you?" I'd say, and hug him tight around the neck. "Always, always go on loving me, and caring for me, so there's no room for anyone else in my heart!" By now his love was all I had to rely on. Over and over I kept saying: "Love me more, more. . . ."

One evening I was so overwrought I must have seemed out of my wits. "You still don't love me enough!" I cried.

My husband tried to soothe me. "You go from one extreme to the other," he said, evidently bewildered by the way I had lost my head.

My worst fear was that Mitsuko might suddenly turn up at my house one day and I would find myself forced to talk to her, whether I wanted to or not. But fortunately, brazen as she was, she didn't seem to have the nerve to come. In my heart I prayed thankfully to the gods and Buddha, grateful that things had turned out the way they did. Really, except for what had happened that dreadful night, I would never have been able to make

such a clean break with her—even *that* seemed to be the
will of the gods.

▼

At last I had become more composed, telling myself
that all the pain and wretchedness was over, I should just
think of it as a bad dream.... It was mid-June, about two
weeks after that night, and people were beginning to
come to the beach in front of our house to swim—the
summer rains had held off the year before, and there was
sunshine day after day. My husband usually had nothing
to do, but for once he had been asked to take a case, and
he kept saying that it would soon be finished, and we
ought to think about going off on a vacation. Then one
day, while I was in the kitchen making cherry jelly, the
maid came in to say there was a telephone call for me
from the SK Hospital in Osaka.

Something or other made me suspicious, and I said:
"I wonder who could be in the hospital. Please go back
and ask who is calling."

"It's not a patient," Kiyo said. "It's a man from the
hospital, I think, and he wants to talk to you himself."

"Oh? That's strange." I felt uneasy when I went to
the telephone, and my hand trembled as I held the
receiver.

"Is this Mrs. Kakiuchi?" the man on the line inquired
two or three times, and then, after making sure, abruptly
dropped to a low voice and asked a curious question.
"I'm sorry to have to bother you about this, but did you
happen to lend a book in English on birth control to a
Mrs. Nakagawa?"

"Well, yes, I did lend someone a book like that, but I don't really know Mrs. Nakagawa. Maybe the person who borrowed it from me lent it to her."

"I see," the low voice replied immediately. "Wasn't the person you lent it to Miss Tokumitsu Mitsuko?"

Actually, I had been expecting that question, but the moment I heard her name, it was as if an electric current surged through my body. Yes, I had lent the book to Mitsuko about a month before, after she told me her friend Mrs. Nakagawa was determined not to have a baby.

"Sister, you must be practicing some good method of birth control, aren't you?" she asked me.

"To tell the truth, I have an excellent book about it," I told her. "It was published in the United States, and you'll find it describes any number of methods." I lent the book to her there and then, and forgot all about Mrs. Nakagawa.

Somehow, though, that book had caused serious trouble at the hospital. He couldn't tell me any more over the phone, but young Miss Tokumitsu was involved in the matter and was so worried that she felt she had to come to ask my confidential advice. She was especially distressed because I had never replied to the many letters she sent me. So wouldn't I please meet with Miss Tokumitsu as soon as possible. For certain reasons, it would be improper for a member of the hospital staff to call on me directly. The best thing would be to talk to Miss Tokumitsu myself and let the hospital remain officially uninvolved. If I didn't agree to that, he said, the hospital couldn't take responsibility for whatever difficulties it might cause me.

I had a suspicion that Mitsuko and Watanuki might have hatched up another plot. Still, it was true that the papers were full of stories about abortion incidents at that time, stories about a doctor being arrested, or a hospital coming under fire. As I said, my book described all kinds of methods—illegal medicines or various mechanical means—and I could easily imagine that Mrs. Nakagawa might have committed some blunder an untrained person couldn't cope with and had had to be taken to a hospital. And because I had told my maid never to show me any letters from Mitsuko, just destroy them all, I wouldn't have known anything about the situation. The man at the hospital sounded very urgent and said that it was imperative I see her that same day.

I phoned my husband about it, and he advised me: "The way things are, you really can't refuse."

So I let them know I was willing to talk to her, and I was told that the hospital would have Mitsuko come to see me right away.

13

IT WAS AROUND two o'clock when I received their phone call, and only half an hour later Mitsuko arrived. Even if the hospital wanted her to come immediately, I knew Mitsuko always took an hour or two to get ready to go out, and I certainly didn't expect her so early that afternoon. But there was the shrill of the gate bell and the clatter of sandals on the concrete entranceway.... All the doors in the house were wide open, and down the corridor, wafted in from the front door on a puff of breeze, came a familiar fragrance. Unfortunately my husband wasn't yet home, and I stood there motionless, confused, wondering how I could possibly escape.

Kiyo had answered the door, and now I heard her call my name as she came running in. She looked pale.

"I know, I know, it's Mitsuko, isn't it?" I said, and I was about to go to meet her. But then I hesitated, not quite knowing what to do, and went on distractedly: "Just a moment . . . well, ask her to wait in the parlor."

After that I hurried upstairs to lie on the bed for a while to calm my pounding heart. At last I got up, daubed on a coat of rouge to hide my pallor, drank a glass of white wine, and resolutely went downstairs.

My heart began beating wildly again when I saw the glint of her boldly patterned kimono through the bamboo shade in the doorway. She seemed to be sitting there drying the perspiration from her face with her handkerchief. Mitsuko glimpsed me through the shade too, and called out "Hello!" with a bright smile, as if she could hardly wait to see me.

"I've hated to let all this time go by without getting in touch, Sister," she said diffidently, watching for my reaction, "but all sorts of things have happened since then. . . . And when I imagined what you must have thought that night, and how angry you must be, I couldn't help feeling awkward about coming." Then she lapsed into her old familiar tone. "Really, Sister, are you still mad at me?" she asked, looking straight into my eyes.

"Miss Tokumitsu," I said, deliberately formal, "I'm not seeing you today on that account."

"But, Sister, if you won't say you forgive me, I can't talk to you at all."

"No, I had a request from the SK Hospital about Mrs. Nakagawa's case, and that's the only thing my husband will permit me to discuss. So please don't bring up anything else. As for what happened that night, it was all because of my own stupidity, and I have no one to blame or be angry with but myself. Only, from now on please don't call me 'Sister.' Otherwise I simply can't have anything to do with you."

At that, Mitsuko suddenly seemed dejected and began twisting her handkerchief into a cord and winding it around her finger. She sat there with downcast eyes, looking almost ready to cry.

"Well, isn't that why you've barged in here to talk to me?" I asked. "Tell me what you have to say."

"If that's how you feel, Sister . . ." She was back to that intimate tone again. "I'll be all choked up—I'm afraid the words just won't come out. But to be honest with you, the phone call you had a while ago—really, it wasn't about Mrs. Nakagawa."

"Oh? Then who *was* it about?"

Mitsuko frowned slightly and gave a little snicker. "It was about me."

Just imagine—how incredibly shameless! To come here looking for my help because Watanuki had made her pregnant! Was there no end to the bitterness she'd have me swallow? I began trembling all over, but I suppressed my feelings and quietly said: "So you're the one who's been hospitalized?"

Mitsuko nodded. "Yes, that's right. At least, I wanted to go into the hospital, but they've told me they can't admit me."

What she said didn't seem to make sense. As she went on with her story, though, little by little, it appeared that she had tried various methods from the book I'd lent her, but none of them worked. If she let it go any longer, people would begin to notice, Mitsuko said, and that had worried her so much that she finally managed to get some medicine from a pharmacist Watanuki knew in Doshomachi, medicine that fulfilled one of the book's prescriptions. And she took it. Of course they didn't tell the pharmacist their secret—they just got the necessary drugs from him and mixed them up as best they could, so perhaps there was some mistake.

Last night she suddenly began to have stomach pains, and by the time the doctor arrived she had already had an awful hemorrhage. He was their family doctor, but when she and Ume explained the circumstances and asked him to take care of her without letting her parents know, he sighed and said: "That's too bad. I really don't see what I can do about it. You definitely ought to have an operation—if you're acquainted with any special clinic, go and ask them for help. All I can offer you is emergency treatment." After that he politely excused himself.

Since Mitsuko happened to know the director of the SK Hospital, she had gone there this morning to ask if they would help her out. But when she was examined she got the same answer: They could do absolutely nothing. It seems the director had had some financial assistance from Mitsuko's father to build this hospital, but when she said what she'd done and pleaded with him to intervene, he simply kept saying how sorry he was.

"A while ago any doctor would take care of a difficulty like this for you," he told her, "but lately we have to be very careful, as I'm sure you're aware. If anything went wrong, it wouldn't only be my problem; your family might be drawn into the scandal, and I could never justify my actions to your father. But why did you let it go so long? If it hadn't come to this stage—if it was at least a month earlier—I might have been able to do something."

Even while he was talking, Mitsuko was having stomach pains and probably bleeding a little now and then, she said, and he must have felt that whatever happened while she was there might cast suspicion on his hospital—so much the worse if he was just looking on passively at her suffering. "Who on earth gave you that advice?" he asked. "Tell me who it was and the kind of medicine you took. If I have to, I'll perform the operation—and I'll do my utmost to keep it private—as long as the person who advised you is willing to be a witness, in case the whole thing gets out."

That's why she told him about borrowing the book from me and all the rest of it, Mitsuko said, and she had mentioned that I'd always been successful following its methods, so she thought it would turn out well for her too. The director pondered for a moment and then said that in a situation like this a doctor wasn't necessary; an experienced amateur could easily see it through. It was commonplace for women in other countries to attend to such matters entirely by themselves, without asking anyone else's assistance. And so if I was all that experienced, it might be best for her to call on me. Anyway, he would be willing to operate, as long as I agreed to take responsibility; if I objected, shouldn't I acknowledge that lending her the book had started all the trouble and it was up to me to help her somehow? Unlike a doctor, I could do it with very little danger of being found out; in any event, it wasn't likely to cause a serious problem for me.

. . . Well, that's what Mitsuko told me he said.

"*Please*, Sister," she begged me, "I hate to ask you to do it, but the longer I let this go, the worse the pains are. It's too much for me, I may get horribly sick, so if you just say you'll take responsibility, I can go ahead and have that operation."

"If I'm to be responsible, what am I supposed to do?" I asked. Either go to the hospital and make a statement witnessed by the director and a third party, Mitsuko said, or else be willing to write something down to be used later, if necessary. But I couldn't do that sort of thing lightly—and how far could I trust Mitsuko? For a person who had had a hemorrhage the night before, she didn't look a bit sick, and it seemed strange that she would be out walking too. Also, she said she'd had a staff member at the hospital call me, but why would anyone like that take part in a scheme to use Mrs. Nakagawa's name? I felt there must be more to it and hesitated to speak out, one way or the other. . . .

But just then Mitsuko cried: "Oh, it hurts! . . . It's hurting again!" And she began rubbing her stomach.

14

"WHAT'S WRONG?"

As I spoke, Mitsuko seemed to turn ashen and sank down, writhing with pain, on the tatami floor. "Sister, Sister! Take me to the bathroom!" she begged. I was anxious and upset and put my arms around her to help her up. Finally she began staggering forward, leaning against my shoulder and gasping for breath.

I waited outside the bathroom door and called in to ask how she was, but her groaning kept getting louder and louder.

"I can't stand it! Sister!"

When I heard that, I burst in frantically. "You've got to be brave!" I cried, rubbing her shoulders. "Has anything come out?"

She shook her head. Then, in a faint, breathless voice as if she really was about to expire: "I'm dying, Sister, I know I'm dying. . . . Help me!" Again she whimpered "Sister!" and clutched my wrists with both hands.

"Oh, Mitsu! How could you ever die from something like this?"

But in spite of my encouragement, she stared blankly up, seemingly barely able to make me out. "You'll forgive me, won't you, Sister? I'd be happy if I could just die here beside you. . . ."

It sounded a little as if she was putting on an act, but her hands did seem to be getting colder as they gripped me.

"Shall I call a doctor?" I asked.

But she refused. "You mustn't. That would only make trouble for you. If I'm going to die, let me die the way I am."

No matter what, I couldn't simply leave her there, so I had Kiyo help me carry her upstairs to the bedroom. Anyway, it was all so sudden that I had no time to spread a futon out for her, and then too, although I had qualms about taking her up to our bedroom, all the doors and windows were open downstairs in the early-summer heat and people could see in, so that wouldn't do. After I put her to bed I meant to telephone my husband and Ume. But she clutched my sleeve hard and wouldn't let go.

"Sister, you mustn't leave me!"

Still, she was a little calmer, she didn't seem to be suffering so much, and I felt a wave of relief. Well, at this rate I won't need to call the doctor, I thought.

The way things were, I couldn't leave her side, so I sent the maid back down and told her to clean out the bathroom right away. Then I thought of giving Mitsuko some medicine, but she wouldn't hear of it.

"No, no!" she said. "Just loosen my sash, Sister."

I undid her sash for her, took off her bloodstained white tabi socks, and brought in alcohol and cotton and wiped her hands and feet. Meanwhile she had started having convulsions again.

"Ooh, it hurts! Water, water! . . ."

She was tearing fiercely at the sheets and pillows and everything within reach, and writhing on the bed, curling her body up like a shrimp. I brought her a glass of water, but she thrashed around violently and wouldn't drink it, so I held her down by force and gave it to her mouth-to-mouth. She seemed to like that and swallowed greedily. Then she cried out again: "It hurts, it hurts! Sister, for heaven's sake get on my back and press hard!" Mitsuko kept telling me where she wanted to be massaged, where she wanted to be stroked, and I kneaded and rubbed away just as she asked. Yet the moment I thought she was feeling better she would utter an agonizing groan—it seemed she might never recover. And when she had even a brief respite she would weep bitterly and say, as if to herself: "Ah, I'm being punished for what I did to you, Sister. . . . I wonder if you'll forgive me after I'm dead."

Soon she seemed to be writhing in worse pain than ever, and she insisted that a clot of blood must have come out. Over and over she cried: "It's coming out, it's out!" But each time I looked, there was nothing of the kind.

"It's just your nerves—I can't see a thing."

"If it doesn't come I'll die! I think you don't care whether you let me die or not."

"How can you say that!"

"Then why won't you help me, instead of letting me

suffer like this? . . . I'm sure you know what to do, better than any doctor. . . ."

That was because I had once told her: "There's nothing to it, if you just have a little instrument." But as soon as she began making all the fuss about it "coming out," I realized that everything she was doing today was only an act. . . . To tell the truth, that had begun to dawn on me gradually, but I had played along, and Mitsuko herself saw I was pretending to be deceived and kept up her own playacting all the more boldly. After that both of us were simply trying to maintain mutual deception.

. . . I'm sure you understand very well what was going on. The fact is, I had deliberately walked into the trap that Mitsuko set up before my very eyes. . . . No, I never asked her what that red stuff was; even now I wonder. Perhaps she smuggled in some of that fake blood they use in the theater.

▼

"Then you aren't still angry with me about the other day, are you, Sister? You'll really forgive me?"

"If you try to deceive me one more time, I *will* let you die!"

"And you won't get away with treating me so coldly!"

In less than an hour we were back on the same old intimate terms, and suddenly I began to be afraid my husband might return soon. Now that we were reconciled, after all that had happened, my need for her was stronger than ever. I didn't want to be apart from her a single moment, and yet as things stood how could we possibly meet every day?

"What shall we do? You'll come again tomorrow, won't you, Mitsu?"

"Is it all right to come to your house?"

"I can't say if it's all right or not."

"Then let's both go to Osaka! I'll phone you tomorrow, anytime you'd like."

"I'll phone you too."

We went on that way till late afternoon, and Mitsuko began getting dressed to leave. "I'm going home," she announced. "That husband of yours will be coming back. . . ."

"Just stay a little longer!" Now I was the one to plead.

"Don't be such a spoiled child!" she said. "You're so unreasonable. I'll call you tomorrow for sure—just be patient and wait till then." She left around five o'clock.

In those days my husband usually came home by six, but although I thought he might be anxious enough to turn up early, it seems that a certain case he'd been working on was keeping him at the office. An hour later he still hadn't returned. In the meantime I straightened up the room, made the bed neatly, and picked up the stained socks that Mitsuko had dropped on the floor— she put on a pair of mine when she left to go home—and as I gazed absently at those red stains, I felt as if I were dreaming. How could I explain all this to my husband? Should I even tell him I'd been up here? Should I keep silent? What could I say that would make it possible for us to go on meeting?

Just as I was revolving those thoughts in my mind, I heard Kiyo call upstairs that the master was home. I stuffed the socks away in a dresser drawer and went down.

"What happened after that phone call?" he asked as soon as he saw me.

"I had a terribly hard time," I said. "Why weren't you home earlier?"

"I wanted to be, but there was some business I had to take care of. What on earth happened?"

"They asked me to come right over to the hospital, but I didn't know whether I should or not. Anyway, I had them let me wait till tomorrow. . . ."

"So Mitsuko left, did she?"

"Yes, but she made me promise to go along with her tomorrow, and then she went home."

"Aren't you at fault for lending her that book?"

"But she told me she wouldn't let anyone else see it—really, I'm in an awful fix! Well, anyhow, I suppose I'll have to go pay a sick call at the hospital. It's not as if I'd never heard of Mrs. Nakagawa. . . ."

With that, I had at least given myself a pretext for going out the next day.

15

THAT NIGHT I could hardly wait for daybreak, and as soon as my husband left the house, at eight o'clock, I flew to the telephone.

"Sister, it's dreadfully early isn't it? Are you up already?"

The voice that came over the receiver was the same one I had heard the day before, but its sweet familiar sound made my heart beat faster than when she had been there with me.

"Were you still asleep, Mitsu?"

"Your phone call wakened me!"

"I can leave anytime now. Won't you come right away too?"

"Then I'll hurry up and get ready. Can you be at the Umeda station by half-past nine?"

"You're sure *you* can?"

"Of course I am!"

"Are you free all day today, Mitsu? It doesn't matter if you're home late?"

"It doesn't matter in the least."

"That's how I feel too," I said.

I got to the station at exactly nine-thirty, but

Mitsuko hadn't come. As time passed, I grew impatient, wondering if she was just taking as long as usual at her makeup or if she had deceived me again. I thought of trying to call her from a public telephone but gave it up, for fear she might come while I was gone and then leave herself.

It was after ten o'clock when she finally came rushing through the station gate and over to me.

"Have you been waiting long, Sister?" she asked, panting for breath. "Where shall we go?"

"Mitsu, don't you know some nice quiet place? I'd like to spend the whole day with no one else around."

"Then how about Nara?" she said.

Yes, of course; it was Nara where we went on that first delightful outing together, Nara that I had to thank for my memories of the evening landscape on Mount Wakakusa. . . . How could I have forgotten a place that meant so much to us?

"That's perfect!" I exclaimed. "Let's go up Mount Wakakusa again!" I was truly happy at the thought of it. . . . As usual when I was deeply moved, tears welled up in my eyes. "Hurry, hurry. Let's go!" I urged her, and my feet hardly touched the ground as we ran to a taxi.

"I was thinking about it all night long, and I decided Nara would be best."

"I couldn't sleep a wink myself last night, but I don't know what I was thinking."

"Did your husband come back right after I left?"

"It was over an hour later."

"What did he say?"

"Let's not talk about it—today I want to forget all that."

When we arrived in Nara we took a bus from the train station to the foot of Mount Wakakusa. This time it was a hazy, hot day, unlike our earlier visit, and we were streaming with perspiration by the time we had climbed all the way to the summit. After that we rested at the little tea shop at the top, and remembering how Mitsuko had rolled tangerines down the hill, we bought some mandarin oranges, which happened to be in season, and both of us rolled them down, startling the deer below into bounding away.

"Mitsu, aren't you getting hungry?"

"Yes, but I'd like to stay up here a little longer."

"So would I," I said. "I'd like to stay up on the mountain forever. Let's just have a snack."

For our lunch, then, we ate a couple of hard-boiled eggs, as we gazed out over the Great Buddha Hall toward Mount Ikoma.

"We picked a lot of bracken and horsetail last time, Sister," Mitsuko said. "Weren't they growing on the hill behind us?"

"At this time of year you won't find any."

"But I want to go over there again," she said.

We walked down to the hollow at the foot of the next hill. Few people had been there even in the spring, and now, in summer, it was utterly deserted, overgrown with rank grasses among the trees, the sort of place you would feel afraid to come to alone. But we were happy that no one else was there, and we found a hiding place among the tall, luxuriant grasses, with only the clouds in the sky to look down on us.

"Mitsu . . ."

"Sister . . ."

"Let's never part again."

"I could die here with you, Sister."

That was all we said to each other, and in the silence afterward I had no idea how long we were there. I forgot time, other people, everything. In my world there was only an eternally beloved Mitsuko. . . .

Meanwhile the whole sky darkened, and I felt chilly raindrops on my face.

"It's started raining!"

"How hateful!"

"We mustn't get soaked. Let's go down before it begins to pour."

By the time we had hurried to the bottom, though, only a few scattered drops had fallen and the rain was over.

"If that's all there was to it, we should have stayed longer."

"What a sneaky rain!"

By then we both felt hungry.

"It's just teatime. Shall we stop in somewhere for a sandwich?" I suggested.

"I know a good place," Mitsuko said, and took me to a new hot-spring inn not far from the station. I had never been there before, but it had all the facilities, private bathing rooms and the like, of the inn at Takarazuka. Mitsuko seemed familiar with it—she called the maids by name and knew the layout very well.

So we spent the rest of the day there and got back to Osaka around eight o'clock. Yet I couldn't bear to part and wanted to follow her no matter where. I went along with her on the Hankyu train all the way to Ashiya, and told her: "I'd love to go back to Nara again! Can you come tomorrow, Mitsu?"

"Shall we make it somewhere closer? How about Takarazuka, since it's been such a long time?"

"That's fine," I said, as I left her. It was almost ten when I got home.

▼

"You're so late I called the hospital a little while ago," my husband remarked.

I was startled but quickly thought of an excuse. "You couldn't find out anything over the telephone, could you?"

"No. They said they didn't have a patient named Nakagawa. It makes me wonder if they weren't trying to hide something. . . ."

"You know, when I tried to go see her, it really wasn't about Mrs. Nakagawa—it was all Mitsuko's doing. Now that I think of it, she looked a little funny when she came here yesterday, but she says she used Mrs. Nakagawa's name because she was afraid I wouldn't have anything to do with her if she asked me herself."

"So Mitsuko was the one in the hospital?"

"She wasn't in the hospital either. I didn't understand any of this and went to ask her to come along to see Mrs. Nakagawa. 'Just stop in for a minute,' she said, so I did, but time went by and she didn't make a move to leave. I urged her to hurry up, and at last she spoke out. 'Actually, I have to ask your help,' she said. 'I meant to tell you when I went to see you yesterday . . . but I haven't been feeling myself lately. I think I'm pregnant. Won't you give me some advice before it's gone too far? I tried reading that book, but it's in English; I can't make head or tail of it, and I'm afraid I'll botch the whole thing.' That's exactly what she told me."

"What an appalling girl! So that's why she had the nerve to make up all those lies to you yesterday!"

"I thought so myself—here she was deceiving me, giving me all that worry—but she said: 'I only lied to you because I couldn't think of any other way out— please don't hold it against me.' Ume came in to apologize too."

"Even so, there are lies and lies. She's altogether too smooth."

"Well, yes, that's true. But there was a man's voice on the telephone yesterday, you know. I'm sure it was that Watanuki. He must have been secretly telling her what to do. Anyway, if it had just been Mitsuko, she wouldn't have made up such a complicated story. I was so furious with her that I said: 'I'm leaving—I won't listen to anything of the kind!' But when I started to go, she clutched me by the sleeve and begged me not to refuse her—if it ever got to her parents, she'd have to give up Watanuki, and then she simply couldn't go on living. She even began to cry. Ume pleaded with me too, said I had to take pity on her mistress and save her life! After all that, I didn't know *what* to do. Finally I gave in."

"Then what?"

"Still, I couldn't afford to be careless about it, so I said: 'I'm not at all sure of those methods. Really, it was wrong of me to lend you that book—how can you think of trying anything so dangerous! You'd better find a doctor you trust. . . .' But before I finished speaking, Mitsuko felt another wave of pain, and we were all upset. . . ."

That's how I poured my story out to him, making up one thing after another and weaving in what happened the day before wherever it would fit. Last night it seems Mitsuko did try one of the medicines she read about in my book, I said, and it was aggravating her condition. I went into some pretty gruesome details, as vividly as if I'd seen it all myself, and told my husband that by this point I felt too responsible to just walk away from the situation. And so I had stayed with her all day, I said, neatly extricating myself from my predicament.

16

"I'LL BE GOING to visit Mitsuko again today," I told him the next morning. "It worries me to leave her alone—anyway, now that I'm mixed up in this, I have to see it through."

For almost a week after that we met every day, somewhere or other, but I yearned for a regular place to spend a few hours alone together, where no one could find us.

"If that's what you want, it's best to be right in the heart of Osaka," Mitsuko said. "You're less likely to be noticed in the midst of a noisy, bustling city.... What about the inn you brought the kimono to, Sister?" she added. "I know the people there, and we'd have nothing to fear.... Shall we try it?"

For me, that Kasayamachi inn held an unforgettably bitter memory—the very mention of it was a calculated attack on my feelings—but in spite of that I said: "Yes, why not? It's a little embarrassing for me, but let's try it." She was well aware of how weak I felt toward her, and I tamely followed her lead; I couldn't even get angry with her.

And yet my embarrassment wore off after the first day. The inn maids soon learned to telephone home for me when I was late in leaving, to give me an alibi. As time went on, we would go to the inn separately and call each other from there. Ume would call us too, if anything seemed urgent. . . . Not only that, but Mitsuko's mother and their other maids all seemed to know the phone number and would sometimes call us. She must have really had them fooled at home, I thought. Once when I went to Kasayamachi early and was waiting for Mitsuko, I happened to overhear one of the inn maids talking on the telephone.

"Yes, that's right," she was saying. "No, we've been expecting her, but she hasn't come yet. . . . Yes. Yes, I'll give her the message. . . . Not at all. . . . We're grateful for your generosity in having our mistress over so often. . . ."

That sounded funny to me, so I inquired: "Was that phone call from the Tokumitsus?"

"Yes, it was," she said, with a giggle.

"And didn't you say 'having our mistress over so often'? Who was *that* supposed to be?"

Again she giggled. "Don't you know, madam?" she asked pertly. "I was talking about *you*, as your personal maid."

When I went on questioning her, I was told she had been instructed to say she was at my husband's office in Osaka.

I repeated all this to Mitsuko and asked if it was true.

"Yes, of course," she replied casually. "I told my family he has two offices, one in Imabashi and one over here, and I gave them this number. Why don't you tell your husband something like that too, Sister? You could say it's a branch of our Semba shop if you want to, or just make up anything you like."

So I found myself sinking deeper and deeper into the quicksand, and although I said to myself I had to escape, by this time I was helpless. I knew I was being used by Mitsuko and that all the while she was calling me her dear sister she was actually making a fool of me.

▼

... Yes, now that I think of it, Mitsuko once told me: "I'd much rather be worshiped by someone of my own sex. It's natural for a man to look at a woman and think she's beautiful, but when I realize I can have another woman infatuated with me, I ask myself if I'm really *that* beautiful! It makes me blissfully happy!"

No doubt that was the kind of vanity that made her want to steal away my love for my husband, and yet I was sure Mitsuko's own heart was drawn to Watanuki. Still, I felt I couldn't stand being parted from her again, and so, jealous as I was, I kept pretending to be confident of her love, never breathing a syllable of Watanuki's name. I'm sure she saw through my pretense. Even though she always called me her older sister, I had become the one to defer to her, as if I were the younger one.

One day when we were together at the inn as usual, she said: "Sister, would you be unwilling to see Watanuki? ... I don't know what you think of him, but he hasn't been able to get over feeling sorry for what happened, and he says he's anxious to meet you again, so that we can all be friends. Eijiro's not a bad person; I believe you'd like him if you got to know him."

"Yes, we ought to get acquainted. It's strange not to have anything to do with each other, and if that's what he says, I'd like to meet him too. If he's somebody *you're* fond of, Mitsu, I'm sure I'll be fond of him myself."

"Yes, I'm sure you will. Then you'll see him today?"

"Anytime at all. But where is he now?"

"He came here to the inn a while ago."

That was what I had been expecting, and I said: "Have him come in, then."

Watanuki promptly joined us.

"Ah, Sister, it's you!" Now he was calling me Sister, though I had been Mrs. Kakiuchi to him the time before. But the moment he saw me he knelt down into a formal posture, as if he felt intimidated. "I can't apologize enough for the other night. . . ."

Anyway, that first meeting had been late at night, when he was in someone else's kimono; this time it was bright daylight, and he was wearing a dark-blue jacket and white serge trousers. I had a different impression—he seemed about twenty-six or -seven, but with an even fairer complexion than I remembered. How extraordinarily handsome! I thought. And yet in fact I found him rather expressionless, pretty as a picture but somehow out of another era.

"He reminds you of that matinee idol Okada Tokihiko, doesn't he?" Mitsuko remarked. Actually, he looked much more feminine than Tokihiko—his eyes were narrow, with rather plump eyelids, and there was something shifty about him, a sort of nervous twitch to his eyebrows.

"Eijiro, you needn't be so ceremonious. Sister doesn't have anything against you."

Mitsuko was doing her best to intercede, but for my part I couldn't warm up to him. I couldn't overcome my dislike for the fellow. Maybe Watanuki sensed that, for he kept to his formal pose, solemn and unsmiling.

Only Mitsuko seemed to enjoy the situation.

"What's wrong, Eijiro?" she said, laughing. "You seem out of sorts. With a face like that, you're not being very polite to Sister, are you?" He was still looking serious as she gave him a meaningful glance and poked his cheek with her fingertip. "Listen, Sister. The truth is, he's jealous."

"That's not so! It really isn't. That's a mistake!"

"It is too so! Shall I tell her what you said just now?"

"And what was that?"

"You said you hated being a man, didn't you? You wished you'd been born a woman like Sister."

"Maybe I *did*—but that's not jealousy!"

Possibly they had planned this silly quarrel to flatter me, but I kept silent, thinking it would be foolish to join in.

"Anyway," Watanuki said, "don't embarrass me like that, in front of Sister."

"Then why not try to be a little more pleasant?"

Finally they dropped the subject, and the three of us left to have dinner at the Tsuruya restaurant. We even went to a movie at the Shochiku on the way home. Still, we didn't seem to feel at ease with one another.

17

OH YES, I forgot to mention it, but when I left the Kasayamachi inn phone number at my house, I said it was where Mitsuko's father's mistress lived.

I suppose that sounds odd—Mitsuko had suggested saying it was a branch of their Semba shop, but meeting at a place like that seemed even stranger. Maybe I should say she was in the hospital, I thought at first, until it occurred to me that she couldn't be staying very long at the hospital, not to mention the danger of my husband's deciding to stop in on his way home from work! Just as I was racking my brain over what to do, Ume came up with this new idea.

We'd have to say that Mitsuko was still pregnant—the medicine she took didn't work, and the doctor refused to give her an abortion—and that as her stomach got bigger and bigger, she finally confessed to her mother and it was arranged for her to be taken in by her father's mistress until the baby was born. His mistress was living at the Izutsu inn in Kasayamachi, we'd say; I would give its actual name in case my husband tried to look it up in the telephone book. He could even come to meet me there.

At this Mitsuko burst out laughing. "I'll have to stuff padding around my stomach before I come to your house!" she said. But that's what we decided, to be on the safe side.

My husband was completely taken in. "So Mitsuko's really pregnant, is she?" he asked, looking quite sympathetic.

"You told me not to get any more involved, you know. That's why I wouldn't help her, no matter what she said. So she has to stay cooped up indoors; she can't set foot outside until the baby is born. It's like being in prison—she's so bored she wants me to visit her every day. What should I do? . . . I'm afraid she might develop a grudge against me. I couldn't sleep at night if I left her all alone."

"I suppose that's true, but it'll make trouble for you if you get mixed up with her again."

"Mm, yes, I thought so too. But this time she's been through so much that she's a changed person. Now she'll *have* to be allowed to marry Watanuki, she tells me, and her family seems to agree. Anyway, nobody goes to see her these days—I'm the only one she has to rely on. Even if it's all her own fault, Mitsuko's in a really pitiful state. 'Listen, Sister,' she says, 'now that I'm pregnant how can anyone have the wrong idea about us? I'll come over one of these days with Watanuki to apologize to your husband, so can't we go on seeing each other like real sisters?' That's all she wants."

He didn't seem ready to accept that. But in the end he let me do as I pleased and only said: "Just be as careful as you can."

From then on I openly received phone calls from Kasayamachi, asking if madam was in, and I called home without hesitation myself; sometimes my husband would call me at the inn around dinnertime and ask: "Won't you be back soon?" That's the way things were going, and I felt that Ume had hit on a good idea.

▼

As for my relations with Watanuki, Mitsuko had managed to bring us together, but we remained wary of each other and wouldn't let down our guard. Neither of us suggested meeting again, and Mitsuko herself seemed to have given up trying to make us friends. Anyway, one day—about two weeks after we all went to the Shochiku, I think it was—Mitsuko and I had spent the afternoon at the inn, but about five-thirty she chased me out:

"Do you mind leaving before me, Sister? I have a little something to take care of."

That was always happening, so I didn't feel particularly annoyed.

"All right, I'll go on ahead of you," I said.

But as soon as I left the inn I heard a low voice calling: "Sister!" When I turned to look, it was Watanuki.

"Are you on your way home, Sister?" he asked.

"Yes, I am. Mitsu's waiting, so hurry on in," I replied sarcastically, and started walking down the street toward Soemoncho to look for a taxi.

"Please . . . just a moment," he called after me, following close behind. "There's something I want to discuss with you. Could we walk around the neighborhood for an hour or so, if you don't mind?"

"I'm perfectly willing to hear what you have to say," I told him, "but she *is* waiting for you."

"Well, maybe I ought to phone her," Watanuki said.

We stopped in at the nearby Umezono tearoom for a snack, and he telephoned Mitsuko. After that we strolled north along the Tazaemon Bridge Avenue.

"I told her some important business had come up and I might be an hour late," he said. "Would you promise to keep our meeting secret, Sister? I can't talk unless you do."

"If I'm told to keep it to myself, you can be sure I will!" I replied sharply. "But sometimes while I'm trying not to break a promise, I find that people are making a fool of me. . . ."

"Oh, Sister. You think Mitsuko acts as she does because I've been pulling the strings, don't you? I know you have your reasons for thinking so." He looked down and sighed. "That's precisely what I want to talk to you about. Which of us do you believe she loves most, you or me? I'm sure you feel you're the victim and that you've been used, but I feel the same way. I admit I'm jealous. According to Mitsuko, having you visit her is just a convenient trick to deceive her parents; that's why she's seeing you, she says. But does she need to do *that* any longer? Isn't it bound to come between us? If Mitsuko loves me, why hasn't she been willing to marry me?"

I listened intently, but as far as I could tell, Watanuki

was deadly serious. And what he said seemed to make sense.

"If she won't marry you it must be because her family is opposed, don't you think? She always tells me she'd like to get married."

"That's what she says, of course. I'm sure her family *would* be opposed to me. Even so, she'd find a way to win them over if she really wanted to. All the more so in her present condition—where else could she go?"

... Yes, from what he was telling me, Mitsuko must have been pregnant after all! I listened with amazement as he went on.

"She says her father is positively furious and would never let her marry anyone who isn't worth at least a million yen, certainly not a penniless, no-account fellow. If she has a baby, they'll send it out for adoption. That's ridiculous! Most of all, there's the poor baby—it's inhuman, isn't it? What do you think, Sister?"

But *he* seemed amazed when I said: "Actually, this is the first I've heard that Mitsu's pregnant. Is she quite sure about that?"

"What? The first you've heard?" He stared incredulously into my eyes.

"Yes, it is. Mitsu hasn't said a word to me."

"But still—she came to see you about an abortion, didn't she, Sister?"

"Yes, but that was an out-and-out lie, just a pretext for trying to get together with me again. When I told my husband Mitsuko was pregnant, I only wanted an excuse to go to see her."

"Oh, is that so?" said Watanuki. Suddenly the color drained from his face, though his eyes looked bloodshot.

18

BUT, SISTER, why wouldn't she tell you she was pregnant? Did she have to lie about it, to you of all people? You really didn't know?"

He kept pressing me, as if he had his doubts, but the fact is that Mitsuko hadn't told me anything of the sort. According to Watanuki, she was already in her third month and had been to see a doctor. In that case, she would have been pregnant at the time she made that scene about hemorrhaging, though at around three months only a doctor could have told her what her condition was—and I had even heard her say from her own lips: "I don't think I could be having a baby." There's no question that she was putting on an act that day, but if what Watanuki said was true, she still might have been trying to conceal her pregnancy from me.

"Did she say why she couldn't have a baby?" Watanuki asked. "Was it because she was following the instructions in that book or because she had some kind of physical condition?"

Of course I'd always tried to avoid anything to do with Watanuki, so I never pursued it with her. . . . And then only the other day she had remarked playfully: "I'll have to stuff padding around my stomach before I come to your house, Sister!"

I couldn't believe she was pregnant, I told him, and he replied that Mitsuko was determined not to get married, but once her pregnancy was obvious to everyone she'd be forced to, no matter what.

"I'm sure she's going to hide it as long as she can," he said.

In Watanuki's opinion, Mitsuko's real preference was for her lesbian lover; she was much more in love with me, and that was why she didn't want to get married. . . . She thought I'd abandon her if she married and had his child, so she kept putting things off from day to day, wondering what to do, whether to try to get rid of the baby she was carrying or to find a way to alienate him. . . .

Maybe it was my own bias, but I simply couldn't believe that she was so much in love with me.

"No, no, it's absolutely true. You're the fortunate one, Sister!" he said. "Ah, it's just the opposite with me—what wretched luck I've had!"

He spoke like an actor in a melodrama and looked almost ready to cry. From the first time we met, I had thought of him as rather effeminate, but when he talked like that, his whole expression and manner seemed unpleasantly womanish, weak but insistent, as he kept stealing sidelong glances at me to see how I was reacting.

No wonder Mitsuko might not be too fond of him, I began to think.

Then Watanuki said that the night their clothes were stolen in Kasayamachi, he didn't want her to call me. She should have had the nerve to borrow a kimono from one of the maids to wear home. She could have told her parents she had become involved with a certain man and it was too late to do anything about it. They could have married right away or just made up their minds to elope, and they would have had nothing to fear. How could she be so shameless as to call Sister at a time like that? Sister, who had no idea what was going on! "Besides," he had said, "surely she wouldn't come even if you called her."

But Mitsuko refused to listen. "I can't go home tonight unless I have the right kimono."

"Then let's run away together!"

"If we do, we'll get in trouble later," Mitsuko had said. "I can talk Sister into it, you'll see. If *I* ask her, she won't turn me down. Even if she's a little mad at me, I'll find a way to get around her." And so she went to telephone me.

"But it seemed somebody else was whispering to her, there by the phone," I said.

"Naturally I was worried, so I went to the telephone with her," he told me.

▼

Before we realized it, Watanuki and I had crossed the Sankyu Bridge and come all the way to Hommachi Avenue. "Let's go a little farther," we agreed, crossing the streetcar tracks and heading toward Kitahama. Up till now everything I had imagined about him had been colored by my feelings toward Mitsuko, and I had seen him as a thoroughly despicable person. But this time he didn't appear to be such a liar, and even that womanish, suspicious manner of his may have been at least partly shaped by Mitsuko—I myself had been warped by all her deceptions. The more I thought of it, the more reasonable it seemed—well, even if he felt he couldn't trust me, still he gave me the impression of being sincere.

Of course I didn't believe that Mitsuko was more in love with me. "You must be mistaken about that," I said, almost consolingly. "Look, Mr. Watanuki, you've just been worrying too much."

"No," he protested. "I'd like to think so, but that's wrong. Sister, you don't know Mitsu's true character."

In his view, Mitsuko was the sort of person who found it amusing to pretend to me that she loved Watanuki, and to Watanuki that she loved me. But her real preference was for me. Otherwise she wouldn't have made up that story about the hospital and come to see me, would she, after we had broken off like that?

"What did Mitsu say when she came to your house?" he asked me. "How did she ever manage to get back together with you? I heard about it later, but I don't know any of the details."

So I told him all about the convulsions and hemorrhaging, to his astonishment.

▼

"Is *that* so?" he exclaimed over and over. "I never dreamed she caused such a commotion! Of course I knew she was pregnant, but I thought she should go ahead and have the baby, so I warned her against trying to get rid of it or doing anything unnatural. I was angry when I heard that she went to ask your advice. But still, even if she did secretly take some kind of medicine, I'm sure she was faking all the pain and hemorrhaging. What do you suppose that so-called blood was?"

It seemed unthinkable to him that she would go to such lengths for a reconciliation unless she loved me. I could see that, but then why did she keep on meeting Watanuki? Wouldn't she have given him up long ago, if she *really* loved me? That puzzled me, but he said Mitsuko would never expose her own vulnerability, no matter how much she was attracted by someone; she'd want to manipulate the other person into falling in love with *her*. Since she was as vain as she was beautiful, she felt somehow deprived unless she was being worshiped. She seemed convinced that it diminished her value to yield to anyone. That's why she was using Watanuki to make me jealous, and to preserve her own superiority.

"One thing more," he said. "She's afraid of what I might do if she talked about leaving me. As matters stand, I don't think she'd dare. But if she ever did, I'd stake my life against it." As he spoke, he stared hard at me with his reptilian red eyes.

19

"IS IT GETTING LATE for you, Sister?" Watanuki asked me. "Do you mind talking a little longer?"

"Not at all," I said. "I'm perfectly willing."

"Then let's go back the same way, shall we?"

We turned back from Kitahama and began walking south, down the same street.

"It's obvious Mitsuko has made us into enemies, and I'm the one who's going to lose out."

"I can't believe that," I said. "Even if Mitsu and I were passionately in love with each other, people would say it's unnatural, so I'd be the one she jilted, if it came to that. Even her family would be sympathetic to you, but nobody would sympathize with me."

"But an unnatural love is to your advantage, Sister. She can find any number of partners of the opposite sex, while there's really no one to take your place. So

I could be thrown over anytime, but she won't jilt you."

... Yes, and he told me that Mitsuko could carry on a lesbian love whoever she married. She could run through one husband after another without the slightest effect on it. Our love, Mitsu's and mine, would endure beyond the love of any husband and wife.

"Ah, how unlucky I am!" he sighed, once again in that melodramatic style. Then he thought for a moment and went on quietly: "Please, Sister, be honest with me. Would you rather see Mitsu take me as her husband, or another man?"

Clearly, from my point of view, if Mitsuko married anyone I'd prefer to have her marry Watanuki, who already knew of our relationship. That's what I told him.

"Then there's no reason for us to be enemies, is there?"

From now on let's join forces, he said. If we stop being jealous and work together, neither one of us will be victimized.... It's only because we've been rivals that Mitsuko could manipulate us any way she pleased. Why not begin getting together in private now and then, to keep in touch? Of course that means we should come to a complete understanding; it wouldn't do to misinterpret each other's positions. He wasn't just parroting Mitsuko's excuses, he assured me, but it seemed foolish to be jealous, when you consider how different homosexual love is from heterosexual. It would be a fatal mistake to try to monopolize the love of such a dazzlingly beautiful woman. Even to share it between us was a luxury, when you could easily imagine five or ten more admirers idolizing her. If he were the only man and I the only woman, wouldn't we be the two happiest people in the world? That's something we ought to agree on, grasping that happiness for ourselves forever, before someone else takes it away.

"How do you feel about it, Sister?" he asked.

"If that's what you sincerely want, I'll promise to go along with it," I told him.

"I'm relieved to hear you say that. Otherwise I'd have made the whole affair public, and that would have ruined everything—not just for myself, even for you! But you're like an older sister to Mitsu, and you can be mine too. I don't have a real sister, so I'll look out for you as if you belonged to my family. Think of me as your very own younger brother, and don't hesitate to confide in me if anything troubles you. Someone like me would be a remorseless enemy, but if I'm on your side I'll give my life for you, Sister. If you make it possible for me to marry Mitsu, I'll do whatever you want, even if it means forgoing my marital rights."

"Would you actually do that for me?"

"Indeed I would! On my honor as a man. As long as I live, I'll never forget my debt to you."

So we walked all the way back to Umezono, shook hands firmly, and parted, after agreeing to meet there whenever anything important came up.

Somehow, once I was on my way home, my heart began pounding out of sheer joy. Did Mitsuko love me that much? Far more than she loved Watanuki? Oh, could I be dreaming? . . . Only yesterday I'd been convinced they were using me as their plaything, and now, suddenly, everything had changed. I felt almost bewitched. Thinking over what Watanuki told me, I had to admit it was unlikely that Mitsuko would have made such a scene if she didn't love me. Why would she even want to see me, if she already had a man of her own? . . . And another thing, going back to when it all started, the time when those malicious rumors circulated about the model for my Kannon portrait: Mitsuko herself must have realized from my behavior how I felt about her. Maybe when she passed me in the street she thought: That girl has an eye for me! She'd watch out for a chance to lead me on. Of course I was eager to strike up a conversation with her, but even though she had kept her distance, her radiant smile lured me into making an approach. And the first time I saw her in the nude, I was the one who took the initiative, but only after being tempted by her seductive manner. . . . All in all, as much as I adored her, when I asked myself how I got into this relationship, I couldn't help thinking I had been affected by those rumors at school, coming just when I was feeling so dissatisfied with my husband. Mitsuko might have perceived that weakness in me and planted the suggestion before I was aware of it. In fact, even the marriage talk with the M family seemed to have been a pretext. . . .

Anyway, I felt that I'd been caught in my own trap, put in the position of making all the advances. Of course I couldn't believe everything Watanuki told me, but maybe he didn't actually advise Mitsuko what to do the night their clothes were stolen; maybe she even had someone else pretend to call from the SK Hospital for her, if the man's voice wasn't Watanuki's—once I began to have such doubts, there was no end to it, and yet, above all, why would she keep her pregnancy secret from me? To be so coldhearted, after making me worry so much—surely that meant she had nothing but contempt for me. Or could it be that he had revealed her secret out of a wish to drive us apart? Did he only mean to make a temporary ally of me, so I wouldn't interfere with his plans, and then drop me as soon as they were married?

▼

The more I thought about it, the more I distrusted him. But about four or five days later, there was Watanuki waiting for me outside the inn again.

"Just a moment, please," he said. "I have something I'd like to talk over with you today, Sister. Won't you come along to that tearoom?"

So I went to Umezono with him, up to a quiet room on the second floor, and listened to what he had to say.

"If we don't put our promise to be brother and sister in writing, I'm afraid you'll never really trust me," he began. "It makes me uneasy too, so why don't we do away with all the suspicion by signing a written oath? In fact, I've already prepared a document with that in mind."

As he spoke, he took from his pocket what appeared to be a pair of legal contracts.

. . . Just look at this, please. It's one of the vows we signed that day.

(*Author's note:* It seems worthwhile to give the full text of the document that Mrs. Kakiuchi provided, not only to introduce its contents at this stage in her narrative but also because it will serve to indicate something of the character of the man who drafted it, Mr. Watanuki.)

SWORN VOW

Kakiuchi Sonoko. Born May 8, 1904. Residence: No. XX, Koroen, Nishinomiya, Hyogo Prefecture. Wife of Kakiuchi Kotaro, Attorney at Law

Watanuki Eijiro. Born October 21, 1901. Residence: No. XX, 5-chome, Awajicho, Higashi-ku, Osaka. Second son of Watanuki Chosaburo, company employee

The aforesaid Kakiuchi Sonoko and Watanuki Eijiro, out of consideration for the strong mutual interest which they both have in regard to Tokumitsu Mitsuko, have vowed that from this day of July 18, 1927, forward they will maintain the bond of brother and sister, in no respect different from that of blood relatives, in accordance with the following conditions:

1. Kakiuchi Sonoko will be considered the elder sister, and Watanuki Eijiro the younger brother. This is because Eijiro, though older, is to become the husband of the younger sister of Sonoko.

2. The elder sister recognizes the status of her younger brother as lover of Tokumitsu Mitsuko, and the younger brother recognizes the sisterly love between his elder sister and Tokumitsu Mitsuko.

3. Both sister and brother will be forever united in seeking to prevent Tokumitsu Mitsuko's love from being transferred to a third party. Elder sister will exert every effort to see that her brother and Mitsuko are brought together in formal matrimony. Her brother, even after the marriage, will offer no objection whatever to the existing relationship between his sister and Mitsuko.

4. If either one of the two signatories should be abandoned by Mitsuko, the other will take corresponding action. That is to say, if the brother is abandoned, his sister will break off relations with Mitsuko; and if the sister is abandoned, her brother will break his engagement to Mitsuko. If marriage has already taken place, he will divorce her.

5. Neither party, without the express consent of the other,

will engage in any such action as running away with Mitsuko, concealing their whereabouts, or committing double suicide with her.

6. Both parties, in view of the danger of provoking an adverse reaction from Mitsuko, will keep this compact absolutely secret, so long as they are not forced by necessity to make it public. It is agreed that should either party desire to reveal it to Mitsuko, or to any third person, there is an obligation to consult the other party in advance.

7. If one party should violate this oath, the other party may be expected to inflict severe retribution by any and all means.

8. This oath shall remain in effect so long as neither party has voluntarily severed relations with Tokumitsu Mitsuko.

July 18, 1927

Elder sister Kakiuchi Sonoko (seal)

Younger brother Watanuki Eijiro (seal)

(*Author's note:* The entire main text of the agreement was written by brush in tiny, meticulously formed characters, very carefully spaced, without a single corrected dot or stroke, on two sheets of fine white Japanese paper bound with a twisted-paper cord. Since more than a quarter sheet of standard legal-size paper was left blank, there was no need for such small characters, but no doubt Mr. Watanuki was accustomed to writing in that rather fussy manner. The calligraphy was adequate, for a young man these days unused to brush writing, but hardly surpassed the vulgar competence of a shop clerk's hand. The two signatures at the end had been written by fountain pen, in that second-floor room of Umezono, and here the signature of the widow Kakiuchi was disproportionately large. What seemed particularly repellent were the two seeping brownish stains that

looked like little flower petals impressed below the signatures; two of the same kind of stains were spread
across the seams of the paper, where seals would also
have been applied. The widow's own account will suffice
to explain them.)

▼

"How does it appeal to you, Sister?" he asked me.
"Are these conditions agreeable? If they are, won't you
please sign and seal the document? Of course if you find
anything lacking, don't hesitate to say so."

"An agreement like this is all right, as far as it goes,"
I said. "But what about a child? Wouldn't you and Mitsu
begin to be more concerned about your own family? I'd
like you to take that into consideration too."

"It's covered by the third provision: 'Her brother,
even after the marriage, will offer no objection whatever
to the existing relationship between his sister and Mitsuko.' So you see, I haven't the slightest intention of
sacrificing you for the sake of our family. But if you're
still worried about it, I'll add anything you like to put
your mind at ease. What do you suggest?"

"Since Mitsu has to carry the baby long enough to
be married, I suppose it can't be helped. But I want you
to promise you won't have any more children."

He thought for a moment.

"Very well," he said. "I wonder how to put it. There
are various circumstances . . ."

He was taking into account all sorts of things that
hadn't even occurred to me—look at what's written by
pen on the back of the second sheet. Those are the
conditions he added at that time.

▼

(*Author's note:* On the back sheet of the vow reproduced above was appended the following text, under the heading "Additional Provision":

The brother, after marrying Tokumitsu Mitsuko, will take every precaution to avoid impregnating her. Should there be any suspicion whatever of pregnancy, he will deal with the situation in accordance with the instructions of his sister.

And two further provisions seemed to have been added as an afterthought:

Even in the case of a pregnancy existing at the time of marriage, all necessary measures will be taken to terminate it, if possible, after the ceremony.

If the brother is unable to guarantee that he and his wife will faithfully cooperate in the fulfillment of these additional provisions, he cannot marry Mitsuko.

Here, as well, a pair of brownish stains dotted the paper.)

▼

When he finished writing this, Watanuki said: "Now that we've made things definite, we can both feel relieved. Reading it over, I can see that it's a good deal more to your advantage than mine, Sister. That must show you how sincere I am." And he asked me to sign my name.

"I'm willing to sign it," I said, "but I don't have my seal."

"For a pledge as brother and sister, an ordinary seal isn't sufficient. I'm afraid I'll have to ask you to bear a little pain."

Then, with a knowing grin, he took something from his pocket.

20

"PLEASE ALLOW ME," Watanuki said, grasping me firmly by the hand and drawing my kimono sleeve up to my shoulder. "This will hurt only a moment."

I had thought he would want a fingertip, but he proceeded to bind two handkerchiefs tight around my upper arm.

"You don't have to do that for a seal, do you?" I asked.

"It's not just the seal. We've got to swear a blood oath as brother and sister." He pulled up one of his sleeves, and held his own arm next to mine. "Are you ready, Sister? You mustn't cry out. . . . Close your eyes—it'll be over before you know it."

I was afraid of what would happen if I resisted; besides, there was no use trying to escape. The object gleaming in his hand had terrified me. It was too late! Now my eyes were shut—what was to stop him from slitting my throat? Just as I resigned myself to being murdered, I felt something sharp graze my arm above the elbow, and I almost fainted, as if I might be having a stroke.

"Steady! Steady!" he encouraged me. I opened my eyes and saw that he was holding his arm out to me. "Come, Sister, you drink first." After that ritual was finished, he grasped my finger, bloodied it, and pressed it hard against the paper again and again, making the seals. "You need to seal it here, and here, and here."

▼

I felt deathly afraid of him and meant to keep my promise faithfully, so I locked my copy of the oath up in the cabinet drawer. It troubled me to keep it secret from Mitsuko, but I tried not to give the least hint to her. Still, I must have seemed nervous. The next day Mitsuko darted a strange look at me and asked: "Sister, how did you get that cut?"

"Oh, that," I said. "I wonder. Last night I was eaten alive by mosquitoes; maybe I scratched myself raw."

"That's funny," she replied. "Eijiro has a scratch in exactly the same place."

Now I see what I'm in for, I thought, feeling myself go pale.

"Sister, you're hiding something from me, aren't you? Please tell me the truth about that cut." And she went on: "You're trying to deceive me, but I have a good idea what happened. You and Eijiro made a private pact, without letting me know, didn't you?"

Well, Mitsuko's suspicions were plainly on the right track. There was no use pretending ignorance if she saw through me like that, but although I knew I had turned white as a sheet, I wouldn't answer her.

"That's right, isn't it?" she insisted. "Why won't you admit it?"

As she kept after me, she told me that yesterday Watanuki had come to see her on his way home and she caught a glimpse of the wound on his arm. From that time on, she had suspected there was more to it; you couldn't imagine both of us having identical scratches at the same time.

"Which of us do you really care for, Sister, Eijiro or me?" she asked.

And then: "Since you're keeping it secret, you must think it's something I have no right to know."

Finally, as if she had to get to the bottom of what was going on between Watanuki and me, she said: "I won't let you leave till you tell me!"

She was as calm as could be, but she kept her gaze fixed on me, and there were resentful tears in those enchanting, indescribably lovely eyes. If she had implored me with her eyes alone, I couldn't have resisted their bewitchment. And if she was already so suspicious, there was sure to be a row sooner or later. The longer I kept my secret, the more she would suspect me, I knew, and yet I couldn't simply blurt it out to her without consulting Watanuki.

"Please wait till tomorrow," I begged her.

But she asked why it had to be tomorrow, why I couldn't tell her today. If I had to get permission from someone else, she didn't even want to hear it. She certainly wouldn't cause any trouble for me if I told her in confidence. Nothing less would satisfy her.

So I retorted: "You say all that, Mitsu, but aren't *you* hiding something from *me*?"

"What could I be hiding?" she protested. "If that's how you feel, just ask me—I'll tell you anything you like."

"Really? You're sure?"

"Of course I'm sure. Maybe there's something I haven't told you about myself, but it's not because I'm trying to keep it secret."

"Not even about your physical condition?"

"What on earth are you getting at, Sister?"

"Well, how about the day you came to my house in so much pain? Were you really pregnant?"

"Oh, that time," she said, her face reddening with embarrassment. "But I was putting on an act. I just wanted to see you. . . ."

"That's not what I'm asking. I'd like to know whether you were *pregnant*."

"Well, I wasn't."

"And you still aren't, even now?"

"Of course I'm not. Why are you being so suspicious?"

"I can't tell you why, but I have my reasons."

"Oh, Sister!" Suddenly Mitsuko looked as if she understood. "Sister, I'm sure Eijiro told you I was pregnant, didn't he? That must be it! But the truth is, he isn't *capable* of fathering a child—"

She broke off, teeth clenched, and tears began trickling down her cheeks.

I was shocked.

"What do you mean, Mitsu?" I said, doubting my own ears.

Then she told me, sobbing, that to this very day she had never concealed anything about herself from me, but that Watanuki had a secret he couldn't possibly reveal, and she had respected his privacy, thinking that if the truth came out, it would be humiliating for both of them and terribly painful for him. But she had no sympathy for a person who would slander her behind her back. He was to blame for getting her into this miserable situation, she said; all her troubles were his doing. Still crying, she started telling me about Watanuki from the first time she met him.

▼

It seems that they became acquainted the summer before last, while she was at her family's villa in Hamadera. One evening he asked her out for a stroll and lured her into the shadow of a fishing boat beached along the shore. Since he also lived in Osaka, not far from her, they kept on meeting after summer's end, finding ways to arrange a rendezvous somewhere or other. But then one day she heard a curious bit of gossip about Watanuki from an old friend, a classmate at her girls' school. Apparently her friend had seen the two of them walking together at Takarazuka. And so on an evening when Mitsuko was out on the roof garden of the Asahi Hall, after going to a movie alone, this school friend called to her and came up behind her and tapped her on the shoulder.

"You were out walking with Mr. Watanuki the other day, weren't you?" she asked.

"Oh, you know Mr. Watanuki?"

"Not personally," her friend said. "But he's awfully good-looking, and everybody makes a fuss over him. So he's just right for a pretty girl like you!" And she gave a meaningful smile.

Mitsuko told her they weren't all that involved; they just happened to be on a little excursion together.

"You needn't explain yourself! Nobody would be suspicious of you, with that fellow. Do you know his nickname?"

When Mitsuko said she didn't, her friend giggled. "They call him the 'hundred-percent-safe playboy.'"

Mitsuko had no idea what to make of it, and kept quizzing her to find out. At last her friend told her that Watanuki was rumored to be impotent, a sexual neuter, and moreover there were credible sources to attest to that.

21

MITSUKO'S FRIEND had learned about it because someone she knew had been in love with Watanuki and had asked a go-between to inquire about a possible marriage to his family. But for some reason his parents shilly-shallied, avoiding a direct answer, and when they were urged to give their consent, since the two young people seemed to want very much to be married, they said that for certain reasons they couldn't take a bride for Eijiro. After further investigation, it turned out he'd had the mumps when he was a child, and that had led to inflammation of the testicles. . . . I don't really understand it, Mitsuko said, but I asked a doctor, and it seems that mumps can bring on serious complications. Of course that's only what she'd been told; maybe it was the result of all his dissipation. At any rate, from then on the girl simply couldn't bear Watanuki. . . .

That part of it makes you feel sorry for him, her friend had said, but why did he have to pursue women and try to win them over with his seductive letters? And he not only made wily comments about "an ideal wife" and so on; he'd invite a girl out for a walk and head straight for some secluded, shadowy place. It seems clear now that it was entirely for his own pleasure. To put it in a nutshell, he wore the mask of a lover in order to take advantage of women.

What was even more infuriating was that Watanuki would say: "I think it's wrong to have physical relations before marriage," and would be admired for his fine character. Then he would tell the girl: "Let's keep this our secret." But when she talked about it later to her friends, out of sheer frustration, she learned that others had had the same experience. Watanuki knew perfectly well that he was handsome, very attractive to the opposite sex, and he would turn up boldly wherever women were likely to gather. It was hard to escape his insinuating charms. Still, however passionate the response, he would insist on preserving a chaste, platonic love, which usually led the woman to admire his virtue and idolize him all the more. Then she would be in his power, and after the affair had reached a peak, she would inevitably be jilted.

"Oh? It happened to you too?"

"Yes, yes. Exactly the same thing."

You heard this from everyone—at a certain point he would quietly slip away. Another oddity was that, unlike genuine platonic love, where even kissing would be out of place, there was nothing so chaste about his affairs. None of the women had realized what was going on, but once it was over they all had the same story to tell. They had been jilted in the same way.

"As soon as there was any definite talk of marriage, he would simply disappear," they said.

Of course a few sympathized with him, but Watanuki went on amusing himself with one virgin after the next, unaware of how many women knew his secret. There was always another innocent for him to seduce.

"Mr. Playboy has another conquest. . . ."

"That's nothing to be jealous about!"

To people in the know, he was a laughingstock.

"I imagine you were in the dark about his reputation too, Mitsuko," her friend had said, "so I wanted to warn you. If you think it can't be true, just ask anybody."

"My, what a repulsive man! He hasn't kissed me yet, but I suppose he'd get around to it soon enough."

▼

Mitsuko left it at that, without revealing her own relations with him. But as soon as she got home, she told Ume everything she had heard from her friend and asked if she thought it was all true.

Ume turned the question back on her. "Can't you tell if it's true or false, miss?"

No doubt Ume thought that Mitsuko could hardly fail to know. Still, it was her first romantic experience with a man, and she had no reason to be suspicious when he told her it would never do for them to have a baby. She really didn't know whether to believe her friend or not.

That startled Ume. "Maybe she was just running him down because you and the gentleman make such a perfect couple, like a pair of dolls. Why don't we have somebody look into it for us?"

They hired a private detective to investigate, and, sure enough, he reported that Watanuki had a sexual deficiency. He couldn't say if it was the result of mumps, but it seemed to have existed from childhood. Strangely, though, the detective had discovered that before his involvement with girls like Mitsuko, Watanuki had frequented the brothels of the South Quarter; inquiries there revealed that even veteran women of the quarter, once Watanuki began to visit them, usually fell madly in love with him. It was all very mysterious, however handsome he was, and people said he must have a remarkable technique. For a while he became wildly popular, though none of those women would talk about it. So the rumors spread, and it was only after following up all kinds of leads that the detective learned that Watanuki had at first managed to keep his defect a secret—until a certain woman got wind of it and, because she happened to be an accomplished lesbian, taught him how to satisfy her sexually in spite of his deficiencies. Later it seems they began to call him a "boy-girl," or a "pansy," but around that time he stopped going to the quarter. He never turned up again at any of the teahouses. I saw that detective's report myself, and it was extremely detailed; he had gone into every last thing as thoroughly as possible.

▼

So while Watanuki was amusing himself in the brothel quarter, he must have become self-confident, confident enough to hunt for inexperienced women, which is when Mitsuko was caught in his snare. . . . That's just a guess, but I'm certain it's what happened.

When Mitsuko realized she was being toyed with that way, she felt she couldn't go on living. She told me she had planned to kill herself but made her mind up to confront him with her grievance before she did.

"How about getting properly married?" she asked him one day, to see how he would answer. "I've already had my parents' approval, if it's all right with you."

He immediately became evasive. "Of course that's what I want, but it's a little awkward now. . . . We need to wait another year or two."

"In fact, you can never get married, can you?"

Watanuki turned ashen. "Why not?" he asked.

"I don't know," she replied, "but I've heard some rumors about you."

Now that they'd gone this far, she told him, he couldn't just leave her; she thought they should commit suicide together. But he kept insisting that the rumors were all lies. Then she showed him the detective's report, and he looked crushed.

"I'm truly sorry," he said. "Please forgive me." And then: "I'm ready to die with you."

But by now suicide seemed out of the question, and after she had vented her bitterness, Mitsuko even began to feel sympathetic toward him once more. Finally she agreed to go on seeing him.

I suppose that was because, in her heart of hearts, Mitsuko couldn't stop loving him and wanted to continue their relationship as long as possible. Watanuki must have been aware of it and asked himself why he had to deny his condition, since she knew all that and yet still appeared to be in love. He told Mitsuko that he always expected women to reject him as soon as they discovered his physical limitation, no matter how they had felt before. He knew he had an affliction; still, he didn't think it was such a fearful defect. If that disqualified him as a man, what was a man's essential value? Was it really so superficial? If it was, he didn't care to be a man. Didn't the saintly recluse Gensei of Fukakusa set burning moxa on the very emblem of his masculinity, because it was an obstacle to virtue? And weren't the greatest spiritual leaders of all—even Christ and the Buddha—nearly asexual? Maybe he himself approached a human ideal. In Greek sculpture, for example, you could find an androgynous beauty, neither wholly masculine nor wholly feminine. Even the bodhisattvas Kannon and Seishi had that kind of beauty. When you think of it, you realize that these are the most exalted forms of humanity. He had hidden his weakness only because he was afraid of being abandoned. Actually, wanting to bring children into the world, in the name of love, was just an animal impulse. That would be meaningless to anyone who cherished a spiritual love. . . .

22

. . . YES, once Watanuki began defending himself he
spouted one excuse after another; there was no end to
it. And he declared that if Mitsuko still wanted to die,
he'd be willing to join her in a double suicide, though
he didn't see why it was necessary. If he killed himself
now, the story might get around that he was in despair
because of a physical handicap. That was hard for him
to bear. He was not so cowardly as to commit suicide
for that reason; he wanted to go on living, do important
work, show everyone that he was far superior to the
ordinary run of human beings. If Mitsuko had enough
strength of will to face death, why *not* get married?
Surely she could see there was nothing shameful about
taking a man like him as her husband; she should think
of it as a noble spiritual union. . . . Of course they
might face difficulties, people who wouldn't understand, so it was just as well not to advertise his dis-
ability. Even if there were one or two gossips around,

none of them had any actual proof, and if anyone asked her about him, he hoped she would say he was perfectly normal. . . .

It was terribly contradictory—if he believed he was so superior, with nothing to despair of, wouldn't he act boldly instead of being secretive? But now all he seemed to care about was getting safely married before anyone tried to block them. That was to be their first aim, and to accomplish it they would have to resort to deception. Why let anything stop them, if they knew in their hearts that they were above reproach?

That might work with other people, Mitsuko had said; it wouldn't be so easy to fool her parents. But Watanuki replied that *his* family would be delighted to have a daughter-in-law who understood his limitation; since it was only her parents who would refuse permission if they found out, it was absolutely necessary to conceal it from them. That could be done, if Mitsuko agreed.

"And if they *do* find out?" Mitsuko asked.

"There's no use worrying about it in advance, is there? If that happens, we'll just explain our feelings openly and honestly, and you can say you'll never marry anyone else. Then if they refuse to let us get married, we can always run away and commit suicide!"

Watanuki probably couldn't imagine that his secret was such common knowledge that he'd been nicknamed for it; he must have thought it was known only to a few women in the pleasure quarter and that he had been discreet enough to keep it hidden. In fact, it seemed most unlikely that they could conveniently deceive her parents and proceed with the marriage. Watanuki's own

"parents" were his mother and an uncle who had
become his guardian, he had told her, and so Mitsuko
only needed to call on them, explain the situation, and
say: "One of these days my family may bring you a
formal marriage proposal, and I hope you'll find it acceptable." His mother would be overjoyed, and his uncle
would never do anything to expose him and spoil his
one chance for marriage. But Mitsuko felt that before
her parents made a proposal, they would undoubtedly
look into his background and somehow or other learn
the truth. So rather than cause an unnecessary storm of
protest, wouldn't it be better just to go on meeting
clandestinely for the time being?

Watanuki declared that he had no overriding reason
to insist on getting married, and he himself realized that
it was asking a lot, for someone in his condition; still,
Mitsuko could hardly be expected to remain unmarried
forever, and he couldn't help worrying that he was
bound to lose her. Moreover, everything he had said to
justify himself was the opposite of what he really felt. If
he could, he wanted to take a wife and live like a normal
man—not just to deceive others but to deceive *himself*,
convince himself that he wasn't different in the slightest
from other men. Not only that, he was vain enough to
want to astonish them all by having a rare beauty like
Mitsuko as his wife. So he was eager to marry her, even
spiteful about it.

"You keep making excuses, but I imagine you'd
accept any good marriage offer!"

Mitsuko retorted that she would never marry somebody else, even if her parents demanded it, and there
were no immediate prospects anyway. Before long she

would be twenty-four, free to make her own decision about getting married. Their chance would come, if he'd only be patient a little longer.... Otherwise they'd have no way out but suicide, she said, and at last she got him to agree to wait.

▼

Mitsuko told me she didn't really understand her own feelings around that time, but in the beginning she was just trying to calm him down, hoping to break off with him somehow. Whenever she met him she felt remorseful afterward and thought to herself: What a ridiculous state of affairs! Envied for my looks by other women and yet in the clutches of a man like that. I've got to put a stop to it once and for all! But strangely enough, after two or three days she would be the one to go chasing after him again. Yet if you asked whether she was so much in love, it seems that she despised the very sight of him and thought of him as contemptible, a man without a shred of character. They were getting together regularly, but they were far from friendly; they always quarreled, and the quarrels would begin with the same old stupid accusations, delivered in a voice dripping with suspicion:

"How long do you intend to keep me waiting?" he might say, or "You must have given away my secret!"

Mitsuko herself had no wish to reveal anything so distasteful, so humiliating for both of them, and she didn't need to be admonished by Watanuki. Still, it was impossible for her to keep it from Ume, and that set off a furious quarrel with him.

"How could you tell a thing like that to your maid!"

Mitsuko was not in the least intimidated.

"You're a liar and a hypocrite!" she shot back. "What you say and do are entirely different! There's no real love between us."

At last, cornered and white with fury, he shouted: "I'll kill you!"

"Go ahead and kill me, if you want to. I've been ready to die for a long time." Mitsuko stood motionless, her eyes shut tight.

Watanuki checked his anger.

"Forgive me; I was wrong."

"I'm not as shameless as you are," she told him. "If the truth ever came out, I'd suffer far more than you! Please don't accuse me like that again."

She had him at her mercy. Watanuki could no longer confront her, but that only made him wilier. Behind her back he was all the more suspicious.

▼

Anyway, around that time talk of marriage into the M family began. . . . That was when Mitsuko was going to the Women's Arts Academy, just to get out of the house and have a chance to meet Watanuki, and she told me it was she herself who started the rumor of a lesbian affair with me, by sending anonymous postcards. She did it because he'd been insanely jealous ever since he got wind of the marriage proposal. He swore he wouldn't put up with it and threatened to expose their relationship to the newspapers. Not only that, but the city councilman's family had entered the competition, and they were doing their best to find some defect that would spoil her chance of marriage. Of course she had no desire to marry Mr. M, so she didn't mind losing out, but what she *did* fear was that their investigation might turn up Watanuki's secret and bring that whole story to light. In short, she had purposely spread her own rumor in order to cover up the true situation.

Well, you could say she deceived me just in order to deceive other people. For her part, Mitsuko preferred to be thought of as a lesbian rather than the victim of a dubious "playboy" or a "pansy." She felt she could escape without being pointed out scornfully and becoming everyone's laughingstock. That was how it all started, from a notion that came to her when she heard I was painting a picture modeled on her and saw how I reacted when I passed her in the street. But I took it so seriously, I was so passionate, that before she knew it she was falling in love. I suppose I wasn't totally naïve myself, but my own feelings were incomparably purer than Watanuki's, and she found herself drawn to me—then too, she said, there was an enormous difference between being the plaything of a near pariah and being worshiped by someone of her own sex, even portrayed as a divine Kannon. So from the time she came to know me she recovered her self-esteem, her natural feeling of superiority, and once again the world seemed bright to her. She told Watanuki she was taking advantage of those rumors to throw people off the scent, and she could use her friendship with me as another excuse to leave her house.

Watanuki was not the sort to accept that at face value, although he put on an appearance of agreeing with her. "Yes, that's a good idea," he said. But he must have felt a stab of jealousy and begun watching for a chance to drive us apart. Now it occurred to her that there was even something fishy about the incident at Kasayamachi. All that business about gambling in another room and a police raid might have been fabricated; from the beginning he could have schemed with the employees at the inn to frighten Mitsuko and then to hide all their clothes while the two were fleeing.... The fact was, that afternoon, before coming to my house, Mitsuko had gone shopping at Mitsukoshi and happened to run into him. She told him she was going straight to Kasayamachi after visiting me, and he should wait for her there. Watanuki could see she was wearing one of our matching kimonos. This was his chance: if he could get that kimono away from her, she'd have to telephone me, and that would surely lead to a rift between us. While he was waiting for her at the inn, he could have bribed the employees and told them exactly what to do—Watanuki was fully capable of a scheme like that and had time to carry it out. It was much too farfetched to think that people wearing their stolen kimonos were taken down to the police station, let alone that the police never bothered to call either Mitsuko's or Watanuki's home. But Mitsuko hadn't suspected any such plot at the time and was far too upset to know what to do.

"There's only one way out," Watanuki had declared. "You've got to call Mrs. Kakiuchi and have her bring you that matching kimono."

Watanuki's account had been quite different. But Mitsuko told me she was so flustered that at first she couldn't remember which kimono she had lost. Even after he advised her to call me, she had said: "I can't ask Sister to do that."

But he kept pressing her.

"Shall we run away together, then? Or will you make that call?"

Mitsuko was desperate. She would rather die than go away with him. Utterly at a loss, she ran to the telephone. Even then she could have tried to keep him out of my sight, especially in a place like that, but she was too confused to ask him to leave ahead of her or to have me come to a nearby café.

That was what Watanuki had aimed for when he told her to hurry and make up her mind. Once I had arrived, she said she couldn't bear to see me.

"Just go and hide," he said. "I'll smooth this over for you."

He did everything he could to play the role of Mitsuko's lover and to lead me on with all his explanations and his insidious questions.

"That's exactly what he did," Mitsuko said. "To tell the truth, he didn't know too much about you until then, Sister."

23

"OH, SO HE WAS trying to lead me on, was he?" I asked. "I thought he was mocking me when he said your feeling for me was absolutely sincere."

"Yes, and that was also to make you angry, Sister. I was listening from behind the sliding door, thinking what a liar he was but that nothing he said was going to convince you. . . ."

Mitsuko was furious with him, once she knew she'd been tricked, but he pursued her all the more relentlessly now that there was no one to hinder him. If she accused him of deception, he replied that she was the real liar. "You were deceiving *me* with all your lies, weren't you?" He never stopped holding a grudge against us. "I'm sure you haven't broken off with her over a thing like that," he would say. "You're still meeting her somewhere, probably."

He had already seen to it that we were no longer friends, and yet either he couldn't give up his jealous doubts or else he was only pretending, just being disagreeable.

"Why don't you act like a man," Mitsuko would retort, "instead of going on and on about something that's over and done with?"

"No, no, it isn't over. . . . I suppose you've told her my secret."

Actually, that was what he was most afraid of. If it ever happened, he warned her, he'd have his revenge on us.

"Don't be ridiculous! How could I have told Sister, when I was hiding the very fact that I knew you? But you've seen her; you must have realized it from her attitude."

"No, there was something suspicious in the way she looked at me," he said.

Watanuki was so used to deceiving others that he distrusted everyone—but this time it wasn't just nastiness; he had reason to be suspicious. Since he knew about my relations with Mitsuko, he thought I must know about his relations with her, and I had never shown any jealousy over it simply because I felt safe, because I'd been told he wasn't a real man. Otherwise wouldn't I have exposed them? That was why he had me called to the Kasayamachi inn: so I would see that he often went to such places with Mitsuko and could hardly be a man of doubtful sexuality.

If he had approached her straightforwardly and begged her to break off with me, even Mitsuko would have felt obliged to agree. But once she'd been tricked like that and then accused of betraying him, she had a perverse desire to turn the tables. The thought of how she had let him come between us made her feel all the more attached to me. She wanted to do anything she could to be reconciled, at least to see me again, if only for the last time. But if she went to my house, I'd probably refuse to see her, and anyway, what sort of excuse could she offer? Whatever she might say, my feelings were unlikely to change.

Racking her brains for a solution, she finally remembered that book. . . . Of course the book was of no use to Mitsuko, and she *had* lent it to Mrs. Nakagawa. Once she got her idea, she spent days planning what to do—how to make the phone calls in the name of the SK Hospital, and so on. Naturally she didn't consult anyone; she developed the whole scheme herself. But she decided she needed a man's voice to make those calls, so she took Ume into her confidence and had her enlist their laundryman.

"All my efforts were just to win you back. Now that I think of it, that scene I put on, rolling my eyes and all, wasn't so bad for an amateur!"

Well, she had to admit that her performance was meant to deceive me, but she felt sure I could understand her motive, even sympathize with her, rather than blame her for it.

▼

However, it wasn't long till Watanuki learned about our reconciliation. Mitsuko wanted to show him she had turned his own plot against him; instead of hiding it, she couldn't wait to see how he would behave when he found out.

"You've been getting together with her again lately,

haven't you? Don't try to pretend you haven't. I know all about it."

"Oh, I'm not pretending at all," she replied coolly. "You'd only suspect me anyway, so I thought I might as well see her."

"Why did you have to do that behind my back?"

"It wasn't behind your back. You can suspect me as much as you like, but I won't lie to you—I'll tell you what I did."

"Yes, but weren't you keeping quiet about it up till now?"

"Why shouldn't I? I don't have to report everything I do."

"Even if it's that important? There must be more to it."

"But I told you I saw her, didn't I?"

"Just saying you saw her isn't enough. Tell me which of you made the first move."

"I went to apologize to her, and she forgave me."

"What!" he cried. "Why should *you* apologize?"

"Am I supposed to forget about her, after calling her out to the inn at that hour and borrowing clothes and money? Maybe you could be so ungrateful, but I couldn't."

"I sent everything we borrowed back to her by mail the next day. There's no need to go out of your way to thank such an insufferable woman."

"Oh? And what did you tell Sister at the time? Didn't you bow your head to that 'insufferable woman' and clasp your hands and beg for help? 'I don't care what happens to me,' you said, 'but if you take Mitsuko safely home I'll be forever grateful!' And now you talk like that! In the first place, think how much trouble you'd have caused if the clothes you sent back fell into her husband's hands. No matter what you say, she's somebody who helped us—you don't know the meaning of the word grateful! The more I hear, the more I think you had something up your sleeve that night. . . ."

Watanuki looked startled. "Something up my sleeve? And what would that be?"

"I don't know, but isn't it funny that you were sure we'd broken off for good, even though I hadn't said a word about it? If you thought I'd fall into the trap you set for me, you were wrong."

"I haven't the faintest idea what you're talking about!"

"Well, then, why didn't the police return our stolen kimonos?"

"How should I know, at this late date?" He seemed stung by her question and shrugged it off with an embarrassed grin. "I can't see why you're so upset—you ought to stop grilling me and come out with it."

▼

But Watanuki was not a man to leave it at that. A few days later he brought the subject up again, this time with a touch of flattery.

"Mrs. Kakiuchi must have been good and angry—I wonder how you managed to get around her," he said. "That's something I'd like you to teach me!" And: "You're remarkably clever, for such a sweet-looking girl. . . . The women in the pleasure quarter are no match for you!"

After this rather backhanded praise, she decided she

might as well give in and tell him the whole story of tricking me into a reconciliation.

"Where did you learn to perform that little farce?"

"I learned it from *you*, of course!"

"Don't be absurd! I imagine you've played that kind of hoax on *me*."

"There you are, being suspicious again. I've never done a thing like that before."

"I can't understand why you'd go to such lengths to be on friendly terms with her."

"Didn't you tell her you don't mind? The other day you said we three ought to be friends."

"I only said that because she'd make trouble if we provoked her."

"That's another lie. You were trying to lead her on—I know all about what you were up to that night."

"And I still don't know what you're talking about."

"Listen, even a worm will turn, you know, and people won't let you get away with plotting behind their backs."

"You have no proof that I've done what you call plotting. Aren't you the suspicious one?"

"Suppose I am. But now that it's come to this, I think you've got to go on being friends with Sister, the way you promised! You may not believe me, but I've never said anything unpleasant about you to her. . . ."

Mitsuko was sharp-witted enough to tell Watanuki that one reason she came to me with her outlandish story was to help him conceal his humiliating condition. She wanted me to believe that he was entirely normal. If she went to all that trouble to preserve his reputation, why couldn't he be a little more generous and let the three of them *be* friends from now on? . . . She was touching a sensitive nerve in him, coaxing and threatening by turns.

"As long as I'm meeting you here at the inn, I intend to have Sister come too," she declared. And she told him she didn't ever want him to stick his nose into our relations again—if he did, she made clear, *he* would be the one she'd leave, not me.

After that, he had nothing more to say.

24

"... YOU KNOW, SISTER, as close as we've been, I feel ashamed to confess all this to you, and I've been holding back, thinking it might turn you against me. I couldn't be more miserable. But today I told you everything!"

Mitsuko was lying with her face in my lap, weeping freely, her tears streaming onto me. I didn't know how to console her—the Mitsuko I'd known until that day was radiant, spirited, her eyes flashing with pride, not the sort of person to betray the slightest weakness or bitterness. It was shocking to see that glorious creature lose her self-confidence and collapse in tears. After that, Mitsuko told me she had always been too stubborn to let anyone see her pain, in spite of how depressed she felt, but still, if it hadn't been for me she'd have suffered far more. Thanks to me, she had the courage to endure misfortune; her mood brightened whenever she saw me, and she forgot her troubles. But today at last, for some reason, sadness had overwhelmed her, she could no longer suppress it by sheer willpower, the dam had burst, and the long-pent-up tears had flowed.

"Oh, Sister, please, please . . . you're the only one I can trust—don't let what I've said turn you against me!"

"How could anything turn me against you? I'm glad you were able to come out with it. You can't imagine how happy I am to have you trust me like that!"

Then Mitsuko seemed to relax, but, weeping all the while, she went on to tell me that Eijiro had ruined her life, there was no future for her, no ray of hope, she could only live out her days in misery. She would rather die than marry that man. Couldn't I think of a way for her to break off with him? Please, she begged me, help me find a way out.

"Now that it's come to this, I'll be honest with you," I said. "The truth is, I made a pledge as brother and sister with Eijiro. We exchanged documents spelling out all the details."

And I told her everything that had happened the day before.

"It's just as I thought!" Mitsuko exclaimed. "No matter what you say, he suspects he'll be found out, so he did all that just to make sure of you, Sister. He wants to drag you along with him if he has to give me up. . . ."

That reminded me of how amazed he looked when I told him it was the first I'd heard that Mitsu was pregnant. "The first you've heard?" he had demanded, his eyes bloodshot, the color gone from his lips. "Did she say why she couldn't have a baby? Was it because she had some kind of physical condition?" Then it came to me that in the midst of our talk he had more than once sighed and repeated that melodramatic outcry: "Ah, what wretched luck I've had!"

I had interpreted that sentimental cry as a blatant appeal for sympathy, but maybe, brazen though he was, he had been overcome by his secret grief and couldn't help revealing the sense of isolation that he tried to hide from others. Still, he had been probing me slyly with his questions: "Why wouldn't she tell you she was pregnant? Did she have to lie about it, to you of all people?" And then: "Her father is positively furious. . . . If she has a baby, they'll send it out for adoption."

That was bad enough, but there were all those special clauses in the agreement. "Reading it over, I can see it's more to your advantage than mine, Sister," he had said. "That must show you how sincere I am." And yet if he hadn't been worried about his own prospects, why did he use all that ridiculous language to try to win my confidence? Just when did he expect to take advantage of our vow? Think of these conditions: "Elder sister will exert every effort to see that her brother and Mitsuko are brought together in formal matrimony." And: "If the brother is abandoned, his sister will break off relations with Mitsuko." And also: "Neither party, without the express consent of the other, will engage in any such action as running away with Mitsuko, concealing their whereabouts, or committing double suicide with her."

That last condition seemed to have been what he had his eye on, according to Mitsuko; the others were only added to fill it out. As legalistic as he was, Watanuki hardly needed to go to so much trouble drawing up an elaborate document. But in fact, lately Mitsuko's attitude toward him had been more and more desperate; there was no telling what she would do. So it looked as if all his scheming was out of fear that the situation would soon go from bad to worse.

As for the time the three of us went to the Shochiku Theater, not so long before, it was Mitsuko who brought us together:

"Why don't you meet Sister for once," she had told him, "instead of being so prejudiced against her? Just by talking to her you could tell what sort of person she is and whether or not she knows your secret." She thought it would keep him from saying anything to me in private, but all evening he was strangely morose and silent.

"Do you suppose he was being so quiet because he already meant to approach me behind your back?" I asked.

"I don't know, but he was always afraid I might throw him over and run away with you, Sister."

"I'm sure that once he brought off the marriage he'd have nothing more to do with me. I don't need you anymore, he'd say."

"All that talk about getting married was just to convince himself; he really doesn't believe it's possible. He knows if he tried to force me I'd rather die. But with you there, Sister, he doesn't have to worry about my being stolen by another man, so he'd like us to go on the way we are."

That day, too, Watanuki was waiting for Mitsuko, but she said she hated the thought of seeing him and hoped I could get him to leave. I told her it would only make him more suspicious than ever; things would get even worse. Better not to mention what we talked about that day, and let me help her find a way to break off with him—I'd manage it somehow, even if it killed me! I'd kill *him*, if I had to! Now Mitsuko and I were both crying, but I did my best to encourage her before I left.

. . . Well, judging by the date on the vow—July 18, that is—it must have been the nineteenth, the next day, that Mitsuko and I had our talk. Around then my husband finished up a case that had been keeping him very busy, and he suggested taking a summer vacation.

"How about going to Karuizawa this year?" he asked.

That was the last thing I wanted to do. Mitsuko seems to be feeling awfully lonely these days, I told him; she can't go anywhere in her present condition, and she keeps saying how much she envies me. If we must leave, I'd rather wait till it's cooler and go to the mountains in a place like Hakone, not so far away. My husband looked disappointed, but I ignored him and for another two weeks hurried off to Kasayamachi every morning as soon as he left the house. Anyway, from that time on, Mitsuko was like a different person, gentler, more vulnerable: not just a devastating beauty but now suddenly like a dove under the eye of a hawk, all the more touching, but anxious-looking whenever we met, without even the ghost of her old radiant smile. I felt devoured by anxiety myself, from the fear, much as I tried to deny the thought, that she might do something rash.

"Mitsu," I told her, "at least be a little more cheerful in front of Eijiro. If you're not, he'll get suspicious and there's no telling what he may do. I'll deal with him, I promise you—after I've finished, he won't dare show his face in public! Just bear up a little longer, even if it makes you so miserable."

But how could I attack Watanuki? He was far more skillful at manipulating people, getting them under his control, and I had no idea how to go about it. Even as I spoke out so defiantly, I was wondering what to say if he happened to be waiting for me in the street outside the inn. There was nothing shameful about refusing to honor that kind of deceitful agreement, but still I felt vaguely guilty for having broken my word, and every time I went out I shuddered to think I might hear that repulsive voice calling "Sister" behind me. Fortunately I never did. Once we had exchanged vows, he seemed to feel he had accomplished his aim. That was lucky for me, I thought.

Meanwhile, day after day, Mitsuko kept asking if I couldn't think of *something*. "I can't stand it anymore, Sister!" she would say. At last she came up with the desperate plan of enticing Watanuki to run away with her. She'd tell me in advance where they were going, and then when the time was ripe, after it got into the newspapers and caused a stir, I was to lead the police to them. . . . Watanuki wouldn't venture near her again after *that* experience! And she was quite ready to sacrifice her own reputation.

"He seems to have guessed what we've been talking about, so we'd better act quickly," Mitsuko said.

"If he has, I'm sure he'll come to see me about our agreement. Let's just wait to use your plan as a last resort."

▼

... To tell the truth, at that time I was so worried I almost came to ask *your* advice again. But I didn't have the nerve, and Ume said she didn't know what to do either. Finally I was at my wit's end; I thought I'd have to ask for my husband's help. Maybe I could confess my lies, up to a point, and see if he knew some legal means of protecting us—maybe I could even persuade him to sympathize with Mitsuko.

But then one day while I was at the Kasayamachi inn, my husband suddenly turned up, without even telephoning ahead. It was around four-thirty; he was on his way home from the office. I was with Mitsuko when one of the maids came rushing upstairs, calling my name:

"Mrs. Kakiuchi! Your husband is here! He says he wants to see you both—what should I do?"

Mitsuko and I looked at each other, stunned.

"Why on earth did he come *here*?" I exclaimed. "Anyway, I'll go talk to him—just stay where you are, Mitsu." And I went down to the entrance.

25

"THIS WAS REALLY HARD to find!" my husband
said, standing by the lattice door at the entranceway.
He had just been to the Minatomachi station to see
someone off to Ise, he told me, and as he walked along
Shinsaibashi on his way back, it occurred to him that
the place where Mitsuko was staying must be nearby.
I'd certainly be here too, he thought, and so on the
spur of the moment he decided to drop in. He had no
particular business, but since I was always going there
to visit her, he felt it would be impolite of him not to
stop in while he was in the neighborhood. And he
wanted by all means to pay his respects to Mitsuko and
to inquire how she was getting along. If possible, he'd
like to take us to dinner. Wouldn't she be able to go
out for a little? he asked, as innocent as could be. But
it seemed to me there was more to it than that.

"Lately she's got so big she doesn't want to meet
anyone," I said. "She never thinks of going out."

"Well, in that case, I'll only talk to her a moment."

I couldn't refuse.

"Let me go see how she feels."

"What shall we do, Mitsu?" I asked her, after telling her what my husband had said.

"What *shall* we do, really? . . . What did you say to him, Sister?"

"I told him you were so big you weren't seeing anyone, but he insisted."

"Maybe he has some reason."

"Yes, that's what I think."

"I'd better see him, then.... I was asking Haru, and she suggested tying a piece of sash-filler around my waist and putting my kimono on over it. I think I'll try that—now I really *am* stuffing padding around my stomach!"

Mitsuko borrowed the padding from Haru, one of the inn maids, and told her to have the visitor wait downstairs. I began helping Mitsuko get dressed, and Haru came back up and said: "I asked him to come inside, but he didn't want to. He told me he'd say hello to you at the entrance, since it would only be for a minute or two."

Then we'd have to hurry, we said, and the maid and I hastily finished dressing Mitsuko. If it had been winter, we could have easily fooled him somehow or other, but she was only wearing a thin undergarment and an un-lined kimono of Akashi silk crepe, and we simply couldn't make her look pregnant.

"Sister, what month did you tell him I was in?"

"I forget exactly what I said, but I told him it was noticeable, so you ought to be six or seven months along."

"I wonder if this makes me look like six months."

"The whole thing has to be puffed out rounder."

With that, all three of us began to giggle.

"Why don't I bring some more stuffing?" Haru said, and she came back with towels and other things.

"Go downstairs again and tell him the young lady doesn't want anyone else to see her," Mitsuko said. "Tell him she rarely goes near the front entrance, and ask him to please come in. Show him to the darkest room you have, so I won't be too visible."

After we had kept him waiting about half an hour, we managed to finish making a six-months' stomach for her and went to meet him.

"I told her it didn't matter, but she said she couldn't receive you until she changed to a proper kimono," I explained, looking closely at my husband to see how he would react.

He was sitting there stiffly in his business suit, knees together, with his briefcase at his side.

"I'm sorry to disturb you," he told Mitsuko. "For a long time I've been wanting to come to see how you are, and I happened to be going by just now." Maybe it was only my imagination, but he seemed to be staring at her stomach.

"You're very kind," Mitsuko said. "I'm afraid I've been imposing on Sister." And she murmured a few ingratiating remarks to apologize for spoiling our vacation plans and then said how grateful she was to me for coming to cheer her up. All the while she was delicately screening her stomach with her fan. Haru had been clever enough to choose a room so dim that it seemed to need a lamp even in daytime. Mitsuko was sitting in its farthest corner, and what with that airless room and all the stuffing inside her kimono, she was panting and dripping with sweat. She looked utterly convincing. A first-rate performance, I thought.

My husband promptly got up to leave. "I'm really very sorry to have bothered you," he said. "Please visit us as soon as you're able to go out." Then he said curtly to me: "It's getting late; why don't you come along?"

"Something seems to be up, so I'll go home now," I whispered to Mitsuko. "Be sure to wait for me here tomorrow."

▼

Reluctantly I went along with him from the inn. "Let's take a bus," he said, and we walked to the car stop at Yotsubashi. After that we took the Hanshin train home. All the way, my husband maintained a bad-humored silence; he would barely answer when I tried to talk to him.

As soon as we entered the house he asked me to come along upstairs; without even pausing to change into a kimono, he started marching up the steps. I followed him, ready for the worst. He banged the bedroom door shut behind us and, indicating a chair facing him, told me to sit down. For a while he said nothing and seemed lost in thought, breathing heavily.

I spoke up first, to break the painful silence:

"Tell me, why did you suddenly come to that place today?"

"Mm . . ." Still looking thoughtful, he said: "I have something I'd like to show you." He took a manila envelope from his pocket and spread its contents out on the table before us. When I saw it, I turned pale. How on earth had that got into his hands? "It's definitely your signature here, isn't it?" he demanded, thrusting that written oath before my eyes.

"I want you to know I don't expect to lose my temper over this, depending on your attitude," he went on. "And if you wonder how I got hold of it, I'll tell you. Only, first of all, I want you to make clear whether you actually signed this document or whether it's a forgery."

Ah, I had been forestalled by Watanuki! My copy was hidden away in a locked drawer, so this must be Watanuki's—maybe he had drawn it up just for this purpose! Of course I'd been thinking of having my husband intervene, and even of confiding in him about Mitsuko, but after his surprise visit to Kasayamachi I could hardly tell him that her pregnancy was just a fake. That would only make the lying worse—if I'd known it would come to this, I would have confessed to him at the time!

"Listen, I won't know what to believe if you refuse to talk. Hadn't you better be honest with me?"

My husband tried to suppress his anger. His tone softened, and he said quietly: "Since you don't answer, I suppose I can assume that you signed it."

▼

After that, he began to tell me what had happened. Five or six days earlier, Watanuki suddenly appeared at his office in Imabashi and asked to see him. Wondering what his business could be, my husband had him shown into the reception room and went to talk to him.

"The fact is, I came to call on you today because I have an urgent request to make," Watanuki had said. "Probably you're aware that I am engaged to be married to Tokumitsu Mitsuko, and Mitsuko is already carrying my child, and your wife has come between us and caused all sorts of trouble. Recently Mitsuko has been getting colder toward me day by day; as things stand, I don't know if she'll be willing to marry me. So won't you please speak to your wife about it?"

"How can my wife be causing you any trouble?" my husband asked. "I'm not familiar with the details of the situation, but she tells me she sympathizes with you both and hopes you'll be married as soon as possible."

Then Watanuki said: "You don't seem to understand the actual relationship between your wife and Mitsuko." He was hinting that we were back on the same old terms.

My husband was not inclined to trust a man he had never met before; and it was hard to imagine that a woman who was carrying his child could be so closely involved with another woman. He began to wonder if the man was out of his mind.

"It's natural for you to doubt me," Watanuki went on, "but here is the clear proof." Then he showed him the document.

When my husband read it, he felt distressed that his own wife was still deceiving him, but what distressed him even more was that, quite unknown to him, she and a total stranger had sealed a pledge of kinship. To begin with, it really angered him to think how this fellow, who had exchanged vows with another man's wife, had boldly come in to his office and displayed it to him, without a word of apology, grinning triumphantly, for all the world like a detective who has just got his hands on a damning piece of evidence.

"I think you'll agree that the signature is your wife's, won't you?"

"Yes, I suppose it looks like her handwriting," my husband replied icily. "But first of all I want to know about the man who signed it."

"That is myself. I am Watanuki." He looked as calm as if the sarcasm was lost on him.

"And what are these brownish marks below the signatures?"

Watanuki nonchalantly started to describe the process of sealing the pledge in blood, but my husband angrily interrupted him.

"According to this document, the relations between you and Mitsuko and my wife, Sonoko, are prescribed in minute detail, but there's no consideration whatever for me as her husband. My position is disregarded. Since you are also one of the signatories, you obviously share responsibility for it, and I'd like you to explain *your* role in the matter. All the more so because it appears that this wasn't Sonoko's idea; she seems to have been drawn into it against her will."

Far from showing any sign of shame, Watanuki responded with another self-satisfied grin.

"As you can see in our agreement, Sonoko and I are linked by Mitsuko, and that relationship has always been in conflict with your interests as Sonoko's husband. If your wife had had any regard for you, she wouldn't have formed such a close tie with Mitsuko, and she would never have exchanged a vow like this. That's precisely what I would have wished, but I have no way to prevent another man's wife from doing as she pleases. In my opinion, this agreement recognizing their relationship amounts to a great concession to Mrs. Kakiuchi."

Now he was implying that he resented my husband's failure to control me. There was nothing illicit about forming a bond of kinship, he said, and so he himself felt he had not behaved immorally.

26

AND SO, as much as my husband loathed that document, he decided he had better try to get it into his possession. He felt he was dealing with an irrational person, and there was no telling what a fellow like that would do with it.

"I understand completely," he assured Watanuki. "If everything is as you say, I'll fulfill my responsibilities without any urging. But I'm in the position of having met you for the first time today, and I need to hear my wife's side of the story. So won't you lend me this copy for a while? If I show it to her, she may very well confess. But if I don't, she can be extremely stubborn."

At that, before saying whether he would lend it, Watanuki cautiously put the document down on his lap.

"And what are you going to do if Mrs. Kakiuchi confesses?"

"What I'll do depends on the circumstances. I can't tell you now. I'm not going to accuse my wife just because you asked me to. Please understand that I'm not acting out of *your* interests; I'm acting for the sake of my own honor and the happiness of my family."

Watanuki frowned slightly.

"I'm not asking you to do anything for my sake," he said. "I came to see you because I thought your interests and mine happened to coincide. Surely you must recognize that."

"I haven't time to worry about your interests," my husband then declared, "and I don't want to either. Excuse me, but I refuse to be dragged into this affair by you. I'll deal with my wife as I see fit."

"Oh, if that's how you feel, it can't be helped," Watanuki replied. "The fact is, I have no connection with you myself, so I'm under no obligation to you. But if your wife runs away with Mitsuko, I won't be the only one to suffer. I began to think it would be wrong of me to keep silent, knowing what I do." He peered intently into my husband's eyes. "Once it came to that, you'd be dragged into the affair whether you liked it or not."

"Yes, I understand your concern," my husband said, being sarcastic again. "Thank you for your kindness."

"Thanking me isn't enough! I don't believe you'd be so foolish as to let your wife run off, but just suppose she *did*. What would you do then? Would you resign yourself to it and say good riddance, or would you go after her wherever she went and bring her back home? You've got to make that decision!"

"I can't tell how I'd behave until the time came, and I won't make any promises to others or let them interfere with what I do. All the more so because relations between husband and wife ought to be settled between themselves."

"But still, no matter what happens, you don't intend to divorce your wife, do you?"

Watanuki's officious manner was so exasperating that my husband told him to stop worrying; it was none of his business whether or not he divorced his wife.

But Watanuki kept right on: "No, I suppose you're far too beholden to her family," and "You'd be showing a lack of gratitude, wouldn't you, if you threw her out just because of some indiscretion"—things like that. Probably he'd heard enough about us from Mitsuko to be well aware of our family affairs.

"You're such a fine gentleman I can't believe you'd do anything unworthy of you."

That kind of talk was more than my husband could stand.

"Why the devil did you come here?" he exploded. "Must you keep blabbing on and on about something that's none of your business? I'll do my duty as a gentleman without any instruction from you! But please understand, I can't guarantee it'll serve *your* interests."

"Oh? Well, in that case, I'm sorry but I can't lend my copy to you." Then Watanuki took up the document, carefully reinserted it in its envelope, and put it away in an inside pocket.

My husband had indeed wanted it, but now he decided there was no use pursuing the matter. That would only have shown weakness.

"All right. I won't ask you to lend it to me against your will," he said. "Please feel free to take it back with you. Only, there's one thing you need to understand: since I've been prevented from showing it to my wife, I can hardly accept it as genuine if she denies what you say. Naturally I would take her word over a stranger's."

"Well, doting on a woman is a man's undoing," Watanuki muttered, as if to himself. "Anyway, your wife has a copy; if you look for it, it'll certainly turn up. Of course you needn't really bother to do that. Just have her show you her arm, and I'm sure you'll find the proof still there."

With that ugly insinuation, he politely excused himself: "I'm very sorry to have disturbed you." And he took his leave.

My husband saw him out to the corridor and came back into his office with a sigh of relief, thinking: What a dreadful fellow! But about five minutes later he heard another knock at the door, and it was Watanuki again.

"Hello. I'm sorry to keep bothering you," he said, with a curiously amiable smile. "Could I just have a little more of your time?" For some reason, he seemed an entirely different person.

Startled, and once again repelled by his manner, my husband watched in silence as Watanuki came up to the table, bowed, and, without waiting to be invited, sat down in the same chair as before.

"I was in the wrong just now," he said. "But I'm on the verge of losing the woman I'd give my life for, so I've been blinded by my own feelings and couldn't appreciate how you must feel. I didn't mean any harm by it—please forgive my rudeness."

"Is that what you came back to tell me?"

"Yes. After I left your office I thought it over and

realized I was wrong. Somehow I couldn't rest until I came to apologize."

"That's very kind of you," my husband replied sarcastically.

"Uh, yes. . . ." Watanuki sat there squirming hesitantly, still with that odd forced smile. "The fact is, you see, I came here partly to make that request of you and partly to apologize, all because I'm in such an agonizing predicament that I can't find a way out. Just try to imagine my wretchedness, the tears I can't begin to shed! If you understand how miserable I feel, I'm willing to lend you the document."

"And how, exactly, *am* I supposed to understand that?"

"I'll be honest with you: what I fear most is that you might divorce your wife. If you do, she'll be so desperate she'll cause even *more* trouble, and I'll lose all hope of marrying Mitsuko. Not that I think you're likely to divorce her, but I can't help worrying about Mrs. Kakiuchi running off somewhere with Mitsuko. I'm sorry to have to insist on this, but if you don't keep a strict watch over your wife, she'll be sure to run away one of these days; when that happens, even if you want to forgive her, you may find it's impossible, considering other people's attitudes. Just to think of it makes me feel the danger pressing in on me. It's so bad I can't sleep at night!"

As he spoke, Watanuki bowed over till his forehead touched the table.

"Please, I'm begging you," he whimpered. "That's how it is, though you may think I'm being selfish, just asking for what *I* want. But consider my predicament, and start to take responsibility for controlling your wife. Don't let her get away from you, ever. I know you can't tie her down, maybe you can't prevent her from escaping, but promise me that if she does, you'll go right after her and bring her safely home. If you agree to that, I'll turn my copy of the vow over to you."

And he added: "I don't need to repeat myself. I know you love your wife very much and you'd never divorce her, but I'd like it to come from your own mouth. If you have *any* sympathy for me, can't you please tell me what is in your heart?"

The more my husband heard, the more disgusted he felt. Why couldn't the man simply have said what he meant all along, instead of prying into their affairs and rubbing him the wrong way? What a slippery fellow— changing his attitude with every change in your response. Any woman would be irritated by that, Mitsuko too, no doubt. That was another of his disagreeable traits.

By then my husband was beginning to feel almost sorry for him.

"Then will you swear you'll never make this document public?" he asked. "Will you leave it in my custody as long as I wish? If *you* agree, I'm prepared to accept your conditions."

"As you've seen, our vow itself says it can't be shown to anyone without the prior consent of the other party, but it's clear that Mrs. Kakiuchi has broken faith, so I can do anything I like with it. I could use it to make trouble for both of you. But I'm not a vengeful person, you know; that's why I brought it here, ready to entrust it to you. Anyway, no agreement is more than a scrap of paper unless you're sincere. So go ahead and take it home, if it's any use to you. I'll be satisfied as long as you promise to observe the conditions I've mentioned."

Why didn't he tell me that in the first place? my husband wondered. "Very well, then," he said. "I'll take charge of it for the present."

But as he was about to hand over the document, Watanuki hesitated. "Just a moment, please. I'm sorry to have to ask this, but could you make out a receipt, for future reference?"

My husband agreed, and wrote: "I hereby acknowledge receipt of the following . . ." At which point Watanuki interrupted him.

"Please add a little more to that."

"What do you want me to write?"

Then Watanuki dictated a whole series of requirements:

The undersigned pledges to observe the following conditions so long as he has custody of this document:
1. He will take responsibility for his wife and will see that she does not violate proper wifely behavior.
2. He will not under any circumstances divorce his wife.
3. He will assume the obligation to present the document, or to return it, at any time upon demand of its rightful owner.
4. In case of loss of the document while in his custody, he will not be released from the obligations specified in the first and second provisions until he has given other satisfactory guarantees to its rightful owner.

That wasn't something Watanuki came out with smoothly, all at once. As soon as my husband wrote down one condition, he would ponder for a moment, and say: "Oh yes, please add another one," as the number grew.

What nonsense! my husband thought. That rascal sounds like a cheap shyster. Half amused, he let him dictate whatever he pleased, and wrote it all down. But then he said: "I'd like to add a proviso of my own: 'However, if the document proves to be false, all pledges herein will be rendered null and void.' How about it? You don't object to putting that in writing, do you?"

Watanuki seemed caught off guard and a bit confused, but my husband quickly wrote down the proviso and handed over the receipt. Again Watanuki hesitated, but in the end he reluctantly put down the papers and left.

▼

My husband told me all this in a rush, and then demanded:

"What about it? Didn't you actually sign such a document? If you have a copy of your own, let me see it." Then he quietly waited for me to answer.

I got up without a word, opened the locked drawer, brought out the copy I had hidden there, and, still keeping my silence, placed it on the table before him.

27

"WELL, YOU DO HAVE another copy; so this one *isn't* a fake, is it?"

Even then I kept silent and only nodded. My husband couldn't tell what I was thinking and leveled a suspicious glace at me. "So all of this is true?" he asked.

'Some of it is," I admitted, "but we were lying to each other too."

As I was listening to my husband, I had made up my mind that by now there was no use trying to hide anything more; better for me to strike back at Watanuki by telling the whole story, every last detail, good or bad, whether it showed me in a favorable light or not. I'd let matters take their course—maybe it would turn out better than I feared; it might even be to my advantage.

First of all, I told him about Watanuki's secret. Mitsuko had lied about being pregnant, I went on; and I explained that she had stuffed padding over her stomach the time he called on us, that she had never really gone to live in the Kasayamachi inn, and that I'd been frightened into swearing in blood to that agreement. I told him everything, from how I had been deceived by Mitsuko and Watanuki to how I had deceived *him*. For over two hours I talked on and on, spilling out everything I knew, while he only grunted in response and sighed occasionally as he listened.

"So I can believe what you've just told me?" he asked. "You're sure about Watanuki?" And then: "The fact is, I've been looking into it myself."

▼

The reason why he had pretended ignorance and let the matter lie until now, four or five days after their meeting, was that Watanuki's behavior was so strange that he felt there must be something deeper behind it. He decided to hire a private detective to investigate further before confronting me. But even in Osaka there aren't many in that line of work, and he wound up going to the same one Mitsuko had hired.

"If that's the man you're interested in, I know all about him," the detective had said immediately. "I investigated him once before."

As a result, by evening of the very day Watanuki called at his office, my husband had a full report on him. It seemed such a bizarre account that at first he thought it might be a different man with the same name, but the detective knew about the involvement with Mitsuko, so there was no room for doubt. . . . Still, it raised so many questions that were hard to fathom—questions about Mitsuko's pregnancy, about the place in Kasayamachi, and about my relations with Mitsuko—that my husband decided to have him investigate Mitsuko herself. That report had arrived the morning of our talk, but because he felt rather dubious about it and wanted to have a look for himself, he had paid his surprise visit to Kasaya-machi.

"You already knew Mitsuko had padded out her stomach, did you?" I asked, trying to sound completely open and frank.

At first my husband didn't answer. Then he said: "I can see that today you're being unusually straightforward. But please tell me clearly if that's because you feel remorse for your past offenses. I know you realize without my saying so how dishonorably you behaved. I'm not interested in digging into such unpleasant matters, so all I ask is for you to sincerely resolve to make amends. Of course we don't have to worry about keeping any promises to Watanuki, but I *did* swear to him that I wouldn't divorce you. I can see I've had my own failings. There's some truth to the argument that I neglected my responsibilities as a husband; in fact, it seems to me that I owe an apology to Mitsuko's family, even more than you do. I feel that both of us are to blame for what happened. Above all, how could I defend myself to your parents if this got into the papers? Even then, if it only amounted to a love affair, an ordinary triangle, there might be some room for understanding, and for sympathy, but anyone who read that agreement would have to conclude it was insane! Maybe I'm just prejudiced, but from what you tell me, that slimy Watanuki caused all the trouble; he's the one that's *really* to blame. If neither you nor Mitsuko had been involved with him,

I'm sure it would never have come to this. . . . I wonder how the Tokumitsus *would* feel, if they knew. Up till now I've thought Mitsuko was at fault, that she was a delinquent young girl who was having a bad influence on you, but I imagine her parents would want to tear Watanuki limb from limb! To have such a beautiful daughter, one you could be proud of anywhere, and then see her ruined by a scoundrel like that—they'd have suffered most of all. . . ."

I knew this was a kind of strategy on my husband's part: he was afraid to say anything contrary to my own feelings, which were always so easily aroused, and he was trying to play on my emotions rather than to appeal to reason. Still, the fact that he brought up her parents, and especially that he seemed sympathetic to Mitsuko, couldn't help affecting me, since his words echoed what I myself felt. Tears had welled up in my eyes as I listened.

"Isn't that so?" he asked, looking at my tear-stained cheeks. "It won't do any good to go on crying. Please make up your mind to be honest with me, and this time, for once, just tell me the truth. If you're determined to leave me, I know I can't stop you. But actually, the only one I hate is that man—I think both you and Mitsuko are to be pitied. Even if we finally have to part, and you go your way with Mitsuko, I'll always feel pity for you. I'll suffer a lot myself, but you will too, you know. After all, you can never marry her, can you? You may be free from the bonds of marriage to me, but you can't expect others to forgive you. So it's up to you whether to wait till you're forced to give in to society, after worrying so many people and covering yourself with shame, or to come to your senses before that happens. It's your choice."

"Yes ... but it was my fate that caused things to turn out this way. . . . I'll have to die to make amends!"

My husband was so shocked he all but leapt out of his chair, and I burst into tears again, dropping my head down on the table.

"What can I do now? Everybody will abandon me; I'll never dare show my face in public. . . . Please, just let me die. You needn't grieve over losing such a depraved woman. . . ."

"Who ever said I'd abandon you? If that's what I meant to do, would I be talking like this?"

"I'm grateful to you. But if I turn over a new leaf, what will become of Mitsuko? . . . You yourself said it wasn't her fault, didn't you?"

"Yes, I did, and that's why I want to save you both. . . . Now listen to me: you're making a terrible mistake. Your kind of love won't save Mitsuko. It's not only you I'm worried about. I think it's my duty to explain this whole state of affairs to the Tokumitsu family and warn them to keep a tight rein on her, so that she'll never go near that man again—and won't keep on seeing you either. That would be for Mitsuko's benefit, wouldn't it?"

"If you do, she'll kill herself. . . ."

"Oh? Why would she?"

"She just would. . . . She's been threatening suicide all along. I've barely been able to stop her. . . . So then I'll die too. I'll apologize to everyone by dying."

"Don't be absurd! What sort of apology would that be, causing nothing but heartache for your parents and me?"

28

I PAID NO ATTENTION to my husband. Head down on the table, I sobbed like a spoiled child, and I kept repeating: "I want to die! Just let me die!"

By that point, saying I wanted to die was the best tactic. What else could I do? ... All I thought of was how I could go on seeing Mitsuko the same as before—really, what I feared most was being divorced. Anyway, now that he knew all this, surely our married life would be harmonious. I'd be very considerate of him, if only he would understand my attachment to her and accept it. Watanuki might try to interfere, but now we had both copies of that incriminating document, and no one would believe anything a man like that said. Even if Mitsuko married into another family, who could criticize two such model housewives, however friendly they were? Not only would we be as close as ever, but our relationship would be much smoother. That would be far better than stirring up more trouble. I knew very well that my husband was the kind of man who longed for a peaceful solution. His worst fear was that I might do something rash, and so, deep in his heart, he was more afraid of a divorce than I was. "If you try to tie me down, I really *will* run away!" I would tell him, and then I'd present my demands, little by little. . . . That was more or less what I had in mind, feeling confident that after a few days he would do whatever I asked. So I tried not to antagonize him. No matter what he said that night, I only went on weeping quietly, as if I'd already made a firm decision and was doing my best to hide it. That bothered my husband so much that he stayed by my side until dawn, without a wink of sleep. He even went along with me to the bathroom.

▼

The next day he stayed home from the office and had all our meals brought upstairs, as we sat there watching each other. Sometimes he would look searchingly at me and say: "If you go on like this you'll wear yourself out—get a little sleep and then think things over when your mind is clear." Or: "At least, promise me you'll give up the idea of dying or running away!" But I would only shake my head and refuse to answer. I thought that at this rate I would soon have him where I wanted him.

On the following day, though, my husband announced in the morning that he had to begin going in to the office on business for a few hours, and he insisted that I swear I wouldn't leave the house or make a phone call during his absence. Otherwise he would take me along with him to Osaka.

"I'll go with you," I said. "I'd be worried to have you go out alone."

"Why should that worry you?" he asked.

"If you secretly went to tell the Tokumitsus what you know, I couldn't keep on living."

"I'd never do that behind your back," he declared. "I wouldn't go there without your permission. I'll swear to it—will you swear to me too?"

Then I told him: "If you'll just promise not to do anything mean, I'll wait here patiently for you while you're gone. Please go ahead and take care of your work; don't worry about me. I think I'll rest a little while you're away."

It was around nine o'clock when I sent him off, and I went back to bed for a time, but I was so strangely excited that I couldn't sleep. Besides, my husband telephoned me as soon as he arrived in Osaka, and he kept calling about every half hour, as I paced up and down the bedroom, trying to soothe my nerves, with all kinds of thoughts racing through my mind. Suddenly it occurred to me that while we were struggling day after day in this contest of wills, Watanuki was likely to be up to something—and Mitsuko too: what had she been thinking since I left her the other day? Had she been waiting for me yesterday from morning till night? Anyhow, since my threats about killing myself weren't having the desired effect, why not bring matters to a head, and yet without causing too great a scandal, by going off with her to some nearby place like Nara or Kyoto? Then we could have Ume come rushing frantically to my husband, to tell him: "My mistress and your wife ran off together! Please go after them, or there'll be an awful to-do when her family finds out!" And we'd have her bring him to us just as we were about to commit suicide. . . . Today was our one chance to act—that was what I thought, but because I couldn't go out, I phoned Mitsuko and asked her to hurry over to my house.

"I'll tell you all about it after you're here, so please come right away!"

Then I warned our maid: "You mustn't mention this to the master." And I settled down to wait for Mitsuko. About twenty minutes later she arrived.

As long as my husband kept telephoning me I felt reassured that he was in Osaka, but still, just in case he came home unexpectedly, I had Mitsuko's parasol and sandals taken around to the garden side, and as a further precaution I met with her in the parlor downstairs, so that she could make a hasty departure by the back way. Mitsuko looked pale and anxious. During the time that we were apart, she seemed to have become exhausted. As she listened to my story, tears filled her eyes.

"So you had to put up with all that too, did you, Sister?"

It seems that from the night before, and throughout the day yesterday, she had been bullied unmercifully by Watanuki.

"You and Sister have been plotting against me," he accused her, "so I decided to outsmart you by going to Mr. Kakiuchi's office in Imabashi and telling him all about his wife. That's why he came to Kasayamachi to investigate. Once he took her home like that, there's no use waiting for her to come back anymore!"

29

AFTER THAT, Watanuki had said he was sure Mitsuko knew he had exchanged written vows with Sister. "But by now that's only a scrap of paper—I left my copy with her husband, just to prove what I told him. And here's the receipt," he added, taking it from his pocket to show her.

"There, it's all down in writing: 'He will take responsibility for his wife . . .' " and so on. One by one Watanuki read the provisions to her, but he held the receipt so that his hand concealed the one my husband wanted.

"Now that I have this in writing from Mr. Kakiuchi, we needn't be concerned about Sister any longer, so I'd like you to sign a pledge with me too."

At that, Mitsuko said, he produced what looked like another draft agreement from his pocket. When she read it, she saw that it was full of brazenly self-serving conditions: Mitsuko and Watanuki were to be forever united in body and spirit; she would follow Watanuki in death; if she violated their pledge she would be subject to retribution; and on and on.

"If these terms are acceptable, please sign your name here and affix your seal."

But Mitsuko refused.

"I won't do anything of the kind!" she told him. "I've never heard of demanding pledges the way you do. You just want to blackmail people."

"There's nothing to worry about, as long as you don't intend to change your mind." He tried to thrust a pen into her hand.

"It's not as if I'm borrowing money! Do you think you can tie down a person's feelings with a contract? This looks like another of your nasty schemes."

"And you won't sign it because you *may* change your mind, is that it?"

"Whether I sign or not, one can't foresee the future," she retorted.

"Well, you'll regret it if you don't! I've got all the proof I'd need to blackmail you." As he spoke, he took a photograph out of his wallet and showed it to her. Surprisingly enough, it was a picture of the document my husband had retrieved.

"I thought Mr. Kakiuchi might not be willing to return it," Watanuki said, "so I had the photo made before I went to Imabashi the other day—I'm not the sort of man to be taken in. If I show it to a reporter, along with my receipt, he'll want to buy them both. I don't know what I may be driven to. . . . You'd better listen to me, or you'll be in serious trouble!" he warned her.

"You see!" said Mitsuko. "That's how contemptible you are! But I don't care—go ahead and sell your story to the newspapers, or anywhere you like, and stop bothering me!"

With that, they parted angrily.

And so, Mitsuko told me, she had stayed away from Kasayamachi today in order to avoid looking weak. She was just wondering what to do next, when she got my phone call and responded eagerly.

As long as Watanuki didn't think his relations with her were hopeless, he was unlikely to take any steps that might harm himself too. But now that things had come to a crisis, it was vital to get my husband on our side. We decided to carry out my plan.

"If you'd like to go somewhere nearby, how about our villa at Hamadera?" Mitsuko asked.

That summer only a caretaker couple were living there, and if Mitsuko said she wanted to go to swim in the ocean, and take Ume along with her, she could arrange to stay four or five days without worrying her family in the least. Meanwhile I could slip out of my house to meet them at the Namba station; by the time the three of us reached Hamadera, my husband would discover that I was gone. No doubt his first move would be to telephone Mitsuko's house. As soon as he knew where she was, he would call Hamadera, and we'd have Ume answer the phone:

"Your wife and my mistress have taken some kind of drugs—they're both unconscious! They've left notes behind, so they must have meant to commit suicide! I was just going to call our house and then call you. Please come right away!"

He'd be sure to get there as fast as he could.

Ume's little speech was an important part of the plot, but being in a realistic coma was more important, even for a hoax like this. We had to take just enough medicine so a doctor would say our lives were in no danger and we'd be all right after two or three days of rest. We didn't know the proper dose for that, but Mitsuko was in the habit of taking Bayer sleeping pills, which were perfectly harmless.

"They say even a boxful of these tablets couldn't kill you," she explained, "so if we take less than that, we'll be on the safe side. Though I wouldn't care if I *did* have an overdose, since we'd be together, Sister!"

"I wouldn't care either!" I said.

And so, once my husband had hastened to our bedside, we would have Ume ready with a story for him:

"They're still groggy, as you see, but the doctor says they're out of danger, and now and then they open their eyes; they're mostly conscious by now. Maybe I ought to report this to my mistress's family, but I know she'll scold me if I do, and I suppose Mrs. Kakiuchi will too, so I haven't called them. Please keep it to yourself. Anyway, your wife can't go home tonight—I hope you'll let her stay for a while, as if she's here on a visit, till she's all well again."

After that we could spend a few more days in bed, sometimes acting delirious, talking in our sleep, or waking up and crying, and Ume would advise him to leave us alone if he wanted us to recover fully. He would have to agree.

▼

"When shall we do it, then?" Mitsuko asked.

"It ought to be today. We won't have a better chance, now that I'm in prison like this."

"I want to hurry too, or Watanuki will be after me again."

More phone calls had come from my husband while we were making our plans, and we began to be afraid we might not have time to escape or, if we did, he would discover it before we reached Hamadera. We would need up to three hours from the time we left before he found us, or the plan wouldn't work. At first I thought of calling his office and telling him I wanted to sleep till evening. "Don't wake me," I'd say, and then lock the bedroom door from inside, crawl out the window, and jump down. But we have a two-story Western house, with a smooth wall that doesn't offer a foothold, and the beach in front would be crowded with bathers too; I couldn't do anything like that before all those people. So we talked it over and decided it was better for me to be on my good behavior two or three more days, and then, after my husband and our maid had relaxed their vigilance, I'd make my escape by pretending to go for a swim.

All I had to do was wait a few days until he began to trust me again; then, as he was about to leave for the office, I'd declare: "If I stay cooped up in this house, I might as well be an invalid; let me go have a swim at least. I'll put on a bathing suit and just go to the beach in front of our house." And I'd actually walk out the door in my bathing suit. Ume would be waiting for me at the beach and would have brought something of Mitsuko's for me to put on, preferably a one-piece dress I could slip over my bathing suit, and a low-brimmed hat or parasol to hide my face. The beach would be swarming with people, so no one would notice me, but since I hardly ever wore Western-style dresses in those days, I was even less likely to be recognized, no matter who saw me. We were to meet between ten A.M. and noon—a time when my husband was sure to be in Osaka. Ume was to come three days from now, unless it rained, but if anything went wrong she would come again the following day, on the fourth day, or the fifth, and so on.

▼

That was what we planned. Then we had another good idea: Mitsuko would go ahead to Hamadera on the evening of the second day, and when my husband called her family they would tell him she had gone to the villa yesterday. When he called Mitsuko, she'd come to the telephone herself and say: "Sister doesn't know I'm here, so I don't expect her." He'd think I hadn't gone very far and might even have drowned myself. Before anything else, he'd want to begin a search for me.

A little later, when the time was right, we'd have Ume call him: "Mrs. Kakiuchi just got here—before I knew it, something awful happened!"

We estimated it would be an hour and a half to two hours before the maid went to look for me. After that she would phone my husband in Osaka; he would make his own phone calls and wouldn't get back to Koroen for another hour or so; then he'd spend one or two more hours asking bathers if they'd seen me and searching all along the shore; finally, after that phone call from Ume, it would take him an hour and twenty or thirty minutes to come from Koroen to Hamadera—in all, we would have five or six hours, which was plenty of time for us to carry out our preparations. Only, I felt sorry for Ume, who would have to go with Mitsuko to Hamadera the day before and then come all the way to Koroen by ten o'clock in the morning and wait an hour or two on the beach in the worst of the heat. If by some chance I had to let her wait in vain, she'd need to come back a second or a third day. But Mitsuko assured me I could count on her.

"She likes to do that kind of thing."

We made all the necessary arrangements, down to the last detail, reminded each other to be careful, and Mitsuko left for home. That was around one P.M. My husband came back at almost the same time, just missing her. It was really lucky I wasn't trying to escape today, I thought.

30

...YES, I DID manage to escape on the third day. The weather and the timing were exactly as I had hoped: a little past ten o'clock, I put on my bathing suit and went down to the beach. When I saw Ume, I signaled to her with a glance, and we walked as fast as we could along the beach for about half a mile, not saying a word, before I stopped to slip on a light cotton print dress. Then Ume gave me a handbag containing ten yen, and a parasol to shield my face, as we separated and headed out to the highway. Luckily a taxi came along, and I got in and went straight to Namba. So I reached the villa before eleven-thirty, and Ume arrived half an hour later.

"My, but you were quick!" she exclaimed. "I never thought it would go so well. Now come out to the cottage with me, before we begin getting those phone calls!"

▼

Ume hustled Mitsuko and me off to an elegant little thatch-roofed cottage in the garden, quite a long way from the house. Once inside, I saw that beds had been laid out with pills and water right by the pillows; I changed from the dress into a summer kimono and sat down facing Mitsuko, wondering if I might really die and if this might be my last glimpse of her.

"If it turns out to be a fatal dose for me, would you die too, Mitsu?"

"And you'd die with *me*, wouldn't you, Sister?"

We wept together, our arms around each other.

Then Mitsuko showed me two farewell notes she had written, one to her parents and one to my husband. "Please read them," she said.

I took out my own farewell notes, and we compared what we had written. They were like real suicide notes, especially Mitsuko's letter addressed to my husband: "I cannot apologize enough for taking your precious wife along with me. Please find the strength to resign yourself to fate." When my husband read it, he would surely be so moved that he would forget his bitterness. Even we ourselves, looking at the letters there before us, had to take this seriously. We couldn't help feeling as if we were actually going to our deaths.

After spending about an hour like that, we heard the clatter of garden clogs as Ume came running toward us.

"Miss! Miss! You have a call from Imabashi! Please come out for a minute, if you can."

Mitsuko hurried off to the phone, and when she came back, she said: "Everything has gone beautifully. Now we needn't wait any longer!"

Once again we embraced, trembling with genuine grief, and we swallowed the pills.

▼

It seems I was completely unconscious for about half a day. Later I heard that by eight o'clock that evening I began now and then to open my eyes and stare anxiously around, but I have no clear memory of anything for the next two or three days—only a sensation of nausea, of suffocating, of pressure inside my head, along with a kind of confused vision of my husband sitting by my pillow—and through the whole time a series of dreams, one after another. First of all I, my husband, Mitsuko, Ume—the four of us seemed to be off on a trip somewhere, sleeping under a mosquito net in a room at an inn. It was a little six-mat room, and Mitsuko and I were lying there together, with my husband and Ume on either side of us, all under the same net. . . . That image lingered vaguely in my mind like a scene from a dream, but judging from the look of the room, dream and reality must have been mingled. Another thing I heard afterward was that late that night my bedding had been drawn into the next room, but then Mitsuko opened her eyes and started calling for me deliriously: "Sister's gone! Bring back my sister! Bring her here!" Her tears were flowing, I was told, and they had to bring me back to the same room with her.

That was the room I had dreamed about, but there were other, stranger dreams. Once, I was taking a nap in another room at an inn, as Watanuki and Mitsuko whispered together beside me.

"Is Sister really sleeping, I wonder?"

"We mustn't waken her."

Dozing off from time to time, I could hear snatches of their secret talk. But where on earth was I? It must have been that Kasayamachi inn—unfortunately I was lying with my back toward them and couldn't see the expression on their faces. Even so, I understood what was going on. I had been deceived after all! Only *I* had taken the sleeping pills, I thought, and I'd been deluded into letting myself be put into this condition; meanwhile Mitsuko had called Watanuki here. Ah, how hateful! I wanted to leap up and tear the masks off those liars! But try as I might, my body refused to obey. I wanted to cry out, but the harder I tried, the more frustrating it was. My tongue stiffened and wouldn't move; I couldn't open my eyes. How infuriating! Yet as I was asking myself what *could* I do, somehow I began dozing off again. . . . Still I heard voices talking on and on for a long time. Strangely, though, the man's voice had changed from Watanuki's to my husband's. . . . Why was my husband in a place like this? Was he so intimate with Mitsuko?

"Won't Sister be angry?"

"I think it's what Sonoko's always wanted."

"Then the three of us should be good friends."

Snatches of talk like that filtered into my hearing. Even now, I'm not sure what to make of it. Were they really talking with each other, or was it partly my imagination, shaping reality as I dreamed? . . . And then, if that was all, it might have been simply an illusion, the product of my confused mind. I denied it myself, thinking it couldn't be true, but there was another scene I recalled, a scene I still can't forget. . . .

▼

At first I thought it was another nonsensical dream, but although the earlier dreams slowly faded as the medicine wore off and I began to come to, that scene alone burned even brighter in my mind—there was no longer any room for doubt. Actually, we both swallowed the same number of pills, but it seems that I was unconscious longer. Mitsuko had eaten her fill around eleven o'clock, combining breakfast with lunch, but I rushed out to the beach without a proper breakfast and had absorbed the medicine on an empty stomach. While I was still half asleep and dreaming, Mitsuko had long since vomited up the medicine and fully recovered consciousness.

Later, though, Mitsuko herself told me: "I didn't know what was going on, except that you were supposed to be lying there by my side, Sister." In that case, my husband would seem to be the guilty one. But according to what *he* confessed, it was the afternoon of the second day at Hamadera; Ume went off to the main house, and he was fanning the flies away from my sleeping face, when Mitsuko murmured "Sister," as if in her sleep, and began moving closer to me. Afraid she might waken me, he slipped between us and took her in his arms, lifting her away, and then put the pillow under her head and pulled the coverlet over her.... Convinced that she was fast asleep, he let down his guard and, before he realized it, found himself drawn into an unyielding embrace. Anyway, my husband was like a child, with no experience in such things, so I'm sure he must have been telling the truth.

31

WELL, THERE'S NO USE trying to find out who was
to blame, but it seems that once they made that first
mistake, even though they felt guilty toward me, they
kept on repeating it. Considering all that, I can't excuse
my husband completely, and yet, for my part, I was able
to sympathize with him. I knew we were hopelessly
incompatible, as I'd told him over and over, and so,
just as I was always seeking another love partner, he
must have been unconsciously seeking one too.
Besides, he didn't know how to fill that lack by drinking
and amusing himself with geisha, like other men, and
so he was all the more susceptible to being seduced.
What happened then was like a dam bursting: blind
passion surged up, overwhelming his strength of will
and reasoning powers, and he was far more violently
carried away than Mitsuko. That was why I had no
trouble understanding the change in my husband's
feelings.

But how to account for Mitsuko? Had she really

been almost asleep, acting on a moment's impulse, or did she have some clear purpose in mind? Did she mean to get rid of Watanuki and take up with my husband, causing so much jealousy between us that she could manipulate us any way she liked? Of course it was her nature to want to attract as many admirers as possible, so perhaps she was back to that old habit. If not, maybe it was a trick to win his support. "I can see that it's wrong," she might have said to herself, "but still this is the best way to keep him on our side." It was too complicated for me—you really can't tell how a person as devious as that feels—but I suppose all those motives worked along with that chance moment together.

Anyway, it wasn't till long afterward that they both confessed to me; in the beginning I just lay there in bed feeling vaguely betrayed, without asking myself why. I was half pleased, half resentful, when Ume came to my bedside and said: "Mrs. Kakiuchi, you needn't worry anymore. Your husband knows everything!" Since I obviously wasn't all that happy about it, he and Mitsuko seem to have had an inkling that I suspected them.

▼

On the evening of the third day, the doctor told me: "It's all right for you to get up now."

The next morning, we left Hamadera. At that time, too, Mitsuko made a point of assuring me: "Everything's fine now, Sister. Tomorrow I'll come to your house and talk it all over with you." But she looked a little guilty, and her attitude toward me was curiously reserved. Somehow she and my husband appeared to be in collusion. As soon as he had taken me back to Koroen, he announced that he had to go to his office.

"I have a little work to finish up," he said, and promptly left the house. When he came home after eight o'clock that evening, all he said was: "I've had dinner." He seemed afraid I'd want to talk.

I knew that my husband wasn't good at deceiving anyone, so I felt sure he'd soon come out with something or other. I'd let him stew in his own juice as long as he liked. I pretended not to notice how he was acting, and at bedtime I went straight to bed, ahead of him. He seemed more nervous than ever and at midnight was still tossing and turning as if he couldn't get to sleep. Even in the dark I could tell that he opened his eyes now and then, glancing over stealthily to see if I was really asleep and breathing evenly.

After a while he called out to me and took my hand.

"How are you feeling?" he asked. "Do you still have a headache? If you're awake, there's something I want to talk to you about. . . . You know what it is, don't you? . . . Please forgive me—try to think that it was just our fate."

"Ah, so it wasn't a dream. . . ."

"Forgive me. Please, tell me you do."

As he spoke, I began sobbing. He stroked my shoulder gently. "I'd like to think it was only a dream," he went on soothingly. "A bad dream, one I want to forget. . . . But by now I can't forget it. For the first time, I know what it means to be in love. Now I realize why you were so infatuated. You kept telling me I had no passion, but it seems that even *I* can be passionate! If I forgive you, won't you forgive me too?"

"You say that because you want revenge on me, don't you? You're scheming with her to leave me all alone. . . ."

"That's ridiculous! I'm not a vindictive man! And now that I understand how you feel, why would I want to make you unhappy?"

On his way home from the office that day, he had met Mitsuko and talked over the situation. If only I would agree to it, he'd assume all responsibility for the three of us and would see that Watanuki never gave us any more trouble either. Mitsuko herself would probably come to our house tomorrow, but she felt awkward about it and had said: "Please apologize to Sister for what happened."

That was what he told me, and he added that he wasn't deceitful like Watanuki, so why shouldn't something I had allowed Watanuki be allowed to him too? Of course even if my husband wasn't going to deceive anyone, what worried me was Mitsuko. In his words, "You needn't be concerned, I'm different from Watanuki"—but I was anxious simply because he *was* "different." For the first time Mitsuko had known a real man, and that made it more serious than anything she had experienced before. Suppose she threw me over. She would have a splendid excuse ("It can't compare with a natural love"), and she wouldn't feel conscience-stricken either. . . . If Mitsuko took that line of reasoning with him, how could I resist? In the end my husband might be persuaded to turn around and say: "Let me marry Mitsuko."

"You and I were wrong to get married," he might tell me one day. "We're much too incompatible to be happy together, living this way. I think we ought to part."

If that day came, I could hardly object, what with all my talk about freedom in love. No doubt people would consider it quite proper for him to divorce a woman like me. Looking ahead, I couldn't help worrying about that kind of outcome. But I felt as if it was bound to be my fate.

Still, if I didn't accede to my husband's wishes I might never see Mitsuko again. "It's not that I don't trust you," I told him, "but somehow I'm afraid of what will come of this. . . ." And I sobbed on and on, endlessly.

"Don't be foolish—it's only your imagination running wild! If any one of us has to suffer, we'll all three die together, won't we?"

My husband started to cry too, and we both wept the whole night long.

32

SO THE VERY NEXT DAY my husband began to exert all his efforts toward winning over Mitsuko's family and resolving the trouble with Watanuki. The first thing he did was go to the Tokumitsu house, ask to see her mother, and explain that he was the husband of Mitsuko's close friend, Sonoko, and that her daughter had asked him to come. In fact, Mitsuko was being pursued by an extremely unsavory man. . . . That was how he started off, and then he told her that fortunately the man hadn't been able to damage her daughter's virtue, since he had a certain physical incapacity, but he was a despicable fellow who had spread all sorts of groundless rumors—that Mitsuko was carrying his child, for example, and that she and his wife were lesbian lovers. This man had forced his wife to sign an incriminating document and might even come to them with his threats, but they should have nothing to do with him.

I know better than anyone how innocent your daughter is, my husband had said. Above all, as Sonoko's husband, I can assure you there is absolutely no truth to those vicious rumors about the relations between my wife and Mitsuko. And also, as a friend of your daughter, I'd feel obliged to protect her even if she hadn't asked me to. Won't you please let me handle this? I'll take responsibility for your daughter's safety, so if that fellow tries to approach you, just send him to me. Tell him to go to my office in Imabashi.

To think that love would make a man talk like that, a man who hadn't even known *how* to lie! After winning over Mitsuko's mother, he went to see Watanuki. Here, the matter was settled with money, he said, and he brought home every scrap of evidence, including the photograph of the agreement, which Watanuki had threatened to sell to that newspaper, along with its negative and the receipt my husband had given him. In two or three days he seemed to have cleared up the whole affair, but Mitsuko and I were bothered by the thought that Watanuki had given up so easily. Even if he had handed over the negative, he might have had another copy made; there was no telling what he might do.

"How much did you pay him?" I asked.

"He wanted a thousand yen, but I got it down to five hundred," my husband said, confident that our troubles were over. "He saw that I knew all the tricks he had up his sleeve and that his threats wouldn't work anymore, so he decided to take the money."

Everything had gone according to plan. Ume was the only one who came out badly. "You let all that go on without reporting it to us!" Mitsuko's mother told her, and dismissed her on the spot.

Ume felt bitterly resentful. Well, we *were* thoughtless not to foresee that she'd be sent packing, in spite of all she had done to help us, and so at the time of her dismissal I tried to soothe her feelings by buying her off with a whole raft of gifts. I never dreamed that she might later take her revenge.

My husband told Mitsuko's family they had nothing more to be concerned about. Her father came all the way in to his office to thank him, and her mother came to thank me too: "She's such a spoiled child; I do hope you'll think of her as your own little sister and look out for her. As long as she's at your house, we never worry. I wouldn't let her go anywhere without you."

She had so much confidence in me that Mitsuko, accompanied by her new maid, Saki, who had replaced Ume, came to visit us openly every day. Even when Mitsuko stayed overnight her mother didn't object. All this was going as smoothly as could be, but my own home life was more tense and suspicious than ever, worse than when Watanuki was involved. Day by day our torment deepened. There were various reasons: before, I used to meet Mitsuko whenever I liked at that Kasayamachi inn, and now I couldn't; in any case, neither my husband nor I could go off with her and leave the other person alone. So we had to stay home, where one of us was always in the way, unless the other was tactful enough to withdraw. And yet Mitsuko, who knew just what she was doing, would telephone the Imabashi office before leaving home and say:

"I'm going to Koroen now." Then my husband would promptly return.

▼

Of course we had agreed not to keep any secrets from each other, so she had to let him know. Even so, she could have come earlier, she could have come in the morning, instead of waiting till two or three in the afternoon, when we would have hardly any time together. And my husband always seemed ready to drop his work and hurry home after she called.

"Why do you need to rush home like that?" I would ask. "I never have a chance to talk to her."

Then he would reply: "I thought of staying at the office a little longer, but there was nothing more to do." Or: "When I'm away, my imagination begins to bother me. I feel reassured as long as I'm at home—if you like, I can go downstairs." Or else: "You have time alone with her, just the two of you, and you ought to realize that I don't."

But when I pressed him about it, his answer was different. "To tell the truth, Mitsuko asked me why I didn't come home immediately, as soon as she phoned. 'Sister is the one who really cares for me,' she said. She sounded angry."

Actually, I don't know how much of Mitsuko's jealousy was serious and how much was assumed for effect. But it went to crazy lengths—tears would well up in her eyes if I called my husband "Dear." "You're not husband and wife anymore, so you mustn't talk to him like that," she would say. It might be all right in front of other people, but among ourselves she wanted me to call him something else—"Kotaro-san," for instance. And she insisted on having him call me "'Sonoko-san" or "Sister," instead of "Sonoko" or "Dear."

That was all well enough, but then she brought sleeping powder and wine along with her and said: "I want you both to take this and go to bed. I'll leave after I see that you're asleep." She wouldn't listen to our objections.

At first I thought she was joking, but she wasn't. "This is a special prescription, and it's very effective," she declared, placing two packets of powdered medicine before us. "If you both swear to be faithful to me, prove it by swallowing this."

Could one of them be poison? I wondered. Did she want me to take it and be put to sleep forever?

That was what flashed into my mind, and the more she said, "Go ahead and drink it!" the more suspicious I felt. As I stared into Mitsuko's eyes, my husband seemed gripped by the same terror. Holding an open packet of white powder, he seemed to be comparing it with the color of the powder in my hand, as he looked searchingly at both of us.

Mitsuko became impatient.

"Why don't you drink it?" she repeated, trembling. "Ah, I understand! You've been deceiving me, haven't you?" And she began to cry.

There's no way out, I thought. I'll take it even if it kills me. Then I lifted the packet of medicine to my lips.

"Sonoko!"

My husband, who had been watching me in silence,

suddenly grasped my hand. "Wait a moment! Now that it's come to this, we'll have to trust to luck. Let's exchange packets and take the medicine!"

"Yes, let's count to three and take it together!"

That was exactly what we did.

33

I'M SURE YOU CAN imagine how suspicious of each other, how jealous, this scheme of Mitsuko's made us. Night after night my husband and I were given the medicine, and every time we took it I wondered if I mightn't be the only one who was under its influence. Had he managed to fake it somehow? Maybe he wasn't really being put to sleep after all! That made me want to see if I could just pretend to swallow the stuff and then spit it out, but the fact is that Mitsuko kept such a sharp eye on us that we couldn't get away with anything. At last, probably still fearful of being hood-winked, she announced that she would give us the medicine herself. Standing between our twin beds (she had insisted we replace our double bed), she administered the sleeping powder simultaneously to both of us, as if to avoid any possibility that we might resent her treatment as unfair. She held a packet of medicine in each hand and had us both lie face up and open our mouths wide, as she poured in the powder. Then she took two of those long-spouted drinking vessels—the kind they use for sick people, you know—and, tilting both of them equally at the same time, gave us warm water to swallow down the medicine.

"It works better if you drink a *lot* of water," she would say, and she'd fill the vessels two or three times and pour the water down our throats. I'd do my best to stay awake as long as I could, trying to look asleep, but Mitsuko told us we mustn't turn over, or lie on our side—she wanted us to lie so that she could see our faces clearly. She would sit between the beds, her eyes fixed on us steadily, and test us in all sorts of ways, watching our breathing, trying to make us blink, touching to feel our hearts beating. She wouldn't leave until we were fast asleep.

But how on earth could we have had anything to do with each other by this time? Even if we'd been left entirely to ourselves, neither of us had the slightest wish to lay a hand on the other; we were as passionless a couple as you could find. And yet Mitsuko said: "If you sleep in the same room, you have to take the medicine."

▼

As the sleeping powder gradually became less effective, she would change the dosage and the prescription, so that we were still drowsy from that powerful medicine even after we woke up. Lying in bed with my eyes open, I felt awful: the back of my head was numb, my arms and legs refused to move, I felt nauseous and hadn't the energy to get up. My husband had the same sickly pallor I did. Sighing, with his speech as thick as if he still tasted the medicine, he would say: "If we keep on like this we *will* be poisoned one of these days."

When I saw how he looked I felt relieved, thinking he must actually have swallowed the medicine, but then I began to suspect that I had been tricked again.

"Really, why do we have to take that medicine every night?"

My husband seemed suspicious too. Peering into my eyes, he said: "Yes, why should we?"

"Obviously there's nothing to worry about, is there, even if we *were* in bed together. She must have some other purpose."

"Do you know what that would be?" he asked.

"I have no idea. I suppose you do, though."

"No, I don't. You must be the one who knows."

"If we go on doubting each other like this, there'll be no end to it. Still, I can't help feeling I'm the only one being put to sleep."

"And I feel the same way!"

"But then, you know very well what happened at Hamadera!"

"That's why I feel it's my turn to be deceived."

"Haven't you ever been awake till Mitsu went home? Please tell me the truth."

"Never. And you?"

"After medicine as strong as that I couldn't stay awake if I wanted to!"

"Oh? Then you *did* swallow it?"

"Of course I did! See how pale I am!"

"I'm as pale as you are!"

We were still going on like that at eight in the morning, when the telephone rang, as usual.

"Time to get up!" Mitsuko said.

Rubbing his sleepy eyes, my husband got out of bed. Sometimes he had to go in to his office, but even if he was altogether too drowsy to leave the house, he knew Mitsuko had told him he mustn't stay in the bedroom after eight o'clock, so he would go downstairs, perhaps to sit in the wicker chair on the veranda, and fall asleep there. That way, I could stay in bed as long as I liked, but my husband was so drained of energy that when he did go to the office he couldn't put his mind to his work. He simply wanted to rest. Yet if he took too many days off, Mitsuko would tell him he seemed to want to spend all his time with me, so almost every morning, whether he had business or not, he would leave the house. "I'll be back after I've had a nap," he would say.

That was when I began telling him: "Mitsu doesn't bother about me; she just keeps saying what *you* should or shouldn't do—it proves that you're the one she loves."

But according to my husband, she wouldn't have been so abusive to anyone she loved. "Isn't she trying to wear *me* out," he said, "to paralyze me so that I'll lose all desire and the two of you can do whatever you like?"

Strangely enough, at dinnertime, even though our stomachs were suffering from the sleeping medicine and we had no appetite, we both ate as much as we could, counting each other's bowls of rice and doing our best to cram down food. We knew it was the only way to weaken the effect of the medicine.

"You mustn't have more than a second bowl," Mitsuko would say. "If you eat too much, the medicine won't work!" Finally she sat beside us at dinner and kept a sharp eye on how much we ate.

When I think back on our physical state in those days, it seems amazing that we managed to survive. Every day our weakened stomachs were subjected to large doses of sleeping powder; perhaps because we couldn't assimilate it, our minds were always cloudy, even during the day, as if we hardly knew whether we were alive or dead. We grew steadily paler and thinner, and worse yet, our senses dulled. Mitsuko, though, in spite of tormenting us and even putting a limit on our food, indulged herself in whatever delicacies she liked, and her complexion was as radiant as ever. For us, Mitsuko seemed to shine like the sun: no matter how exhausted we felt, the sight of her face brought us back to life; it was our sole remaining pleasure.

Mitsuko herself remarked: "You seem to feel as if your nerves are numb, but you do brighten up a little when you see me, don't you? Maybe the trouble is you're just not passionate enough." She could tell by the degree of excitement which of us had stronger feelings for her, she said, and that was all the more reason to keep on giving us sleeping medicine. Really, you might say she wasn't interested in being offered an everyday love; nothing would satisfy her unless she felt it was a passion that flamed up even though desire had been blunted by the power of the medicine. . . .

▼

In the end, both my husband and I were like empty husks—she wanted us to seek no other happiness, to live only for the light of our sun, Mitsuko, with no further desires or interests in the world. If we objected to the medicine, she would burst into angry tears. Well, of course Mitsuko had long ago shown how much she liked to test the devotion of her admirers, but she must have had some other reason to carry it to such hysterical lengths. I wonder if it might not have been Watanuki's influence. Had that first experience left her dissatisfied with an ordinary, wholesome relationship, so that she wanted to turn anyone who was in her clutches into another Watanuki? Otherwise why did she need to paralyze our senses so cruelly? In the old tales you often heard of spirit possession, by the dead or the living, but the way Mitsuko behaved, wilder and wilder every day, made you think she herself was under the spell of Watanuki's deep-seated bitterness. It was enough to make your hair stand on end.

And not only that. It wasn't just Mitsuko; even my normal, healthy husband, a man without the slightest trace of irrationality, had changed character. By the time I noticed it, he had already become spiteful and jealous; humoring Mitsuko, with a weird grin on his pallid face, he seemed womanish, crafty, mean-spirited. If you watched closely, everything about him—his tone of voice, the whole way he talked, his facial expression, the look in his eyes—seemed to be the very image of Watanuki. I know a person's face is supposed to reflect what he feels in his heart—but still, do you suppose there really is such a thing as a vengeful spirit's curse? Is that just a foolish superstition? Anyway, Watanuki was so dreadfully spiteful that it was easy to imagine him putting a curse on us and casting some kind of spell to take possession of my husband.

▼

"You're getting to be more and more like Watanuki," I told him one day.

"I think so myself," he replied. "Mitsu wants to turn me into a second Watanuki."

By that time he had meekly bowed to his fate, whatever it might bring. Far from trying to resist becoming another Watanuki, he seemed happy about it; as for the sleeping medicine, eventually he was asking Mitsuko to give him more. And Mitsuko, now that the three of us had arrived at this stage . . . how could there be a satisfactory conclusion for her? She must have felt desperate, ready to do anything, maybe even to weaken us with that medicine until she had killed us off—didn't she have a scheme like that buried deep in her heart? . . . I wasn't the only one who thought so. My husband was resigned to it. She might just be waiting for the day we both dwindled down to wraiths and died, a day not far off, when she would skillfully have freed herself from us and become completely respectable, ready for a good match.

"Mitsu seems to be thriving, but look how sickly you and I are," he said. "I'm sure she has something like that in mind."

By then both of us were so debilitated that we no longer felt the least pleasure; we lived only with the thought that today or tomorrow might be our last.

▼

Ah . . . how happy I would have been if we had died together then, as we expected. What changed everything was that newspaper article. It was around the twentieth of September, I think. Anyway, one morning my husband demanded I get up, to see what somebody had sent us. He spread out the gossip page of a newspaper I'd never seen before, and the first thing that struck my eye was a big photograph of that agreement Watanuki had had me sign, along with the heading (circled twice in red ink) of a long article! And I noticed an announcement that the reporter had accumulated a great deal of material; this was only the beginning of a series of articles exposing the sordid vices of the leisure class.

"Look at that!" I said. "Watanuki tricked us after all!" Yet I felt curiously calm, not in the least bitter or angry. I thought that at last the end had come.

"Yes, but he's a fool!" My husband smiled coldly, the blood draining from his cheeks. "What good does it do him to make all that public?"

"Never mind," I said. "We can just ignore it."

I felt confident that people would find it hard to believe, since that so-called newspaper was really nothing but a scandal sheet; still, I called Mitsuko right away to warn her of what had happened.

"Somebody sent us this paper—did you get one too, Mitsu?"

She hurried out to look, and when she came back she said: "Yes, it's here! Luckily nobody else has seen it!"

Hiding the paper under her kimono, she came straight over to our house.

▼

"What do you suppose we can do about it?" Mitsuko asked.

At first we decided there was no need to be upset. If Watanuki had sold them the material, surely he wouldn't have gone out of his way to incriminate himself; the gossip about my affair with Mitsuko was nothing new either, so it might all blow over without much effect. Mitsuko's family found out about it in another two or three days, but we had my husband assure them that the reports were false.

"It's the same old slander," he told them, "and this time it's gone too far. You could sue the paper for publishing that forged signature."

For the moment we felt relieved. But those articles went on day after day, getting sharper and more revealing and bringing to light even facts unfavorable to Watanuki, along with stories about the Kasayamachi inn, our excursions to Nara, the time Mitsuko put stuffing under her kimono to meet my husband—the reporter seemed to know things Watanuki himself wouldn't have known. At this rate, everything about the Hamadera episode would be coming out, from the suicide hoax to the way my husband was drawn into the whirlpool. Another funny thing was that although Mitsuko and I both locked away our letters, one of the letters I sent her—a terribly violent letter, full of embarrassing expressions—had somehow been stolen and a photo of it boldly published in the paper. Only Ume could have taken it, so we had to conclude that she was in league with Watanuki. In fact, she came to see me two or three times after being fired by Mitsuko's family and loitered around suspiciously, with no particular business. Did she want more money, after everything I'd done for her? I wondered. Finally I just ignored her, thinking it wasn't necessary to trouble myself any further, but she came again a few days before that first newspaper article, said something waspish about Mitsuko, and left. I never saw her again.

"What an ungrateful woman!" Mitsuko exclaimed. "She was never just a servant, all the time she was at my house. I treated her like my own sister. . . ."

"Probably you spoiled her."

"That's what you call biting the hand that feeds you. How could she possibly complain, after all *you* did for her, Sister!"

"She must have been bribed by Watanuki."

Well, it's only a guess, but once the newspaper began to investigate on the basis of Watanuki's information and started ferreting out one secret after another, perhaps they were lucky enough to get hold of Ume. Or else that awful Watanuki had worked with her from the beginning and maybe even sold the reporter his own secrets, out of desperation. No matter what, by this time we didn't have a moment to waste. If we kept hesitating, sooner or later Mitsuko would be confined to her house, so she wanted us to go ahead with the plan we had agreed upon. Still, days went by, one after another, as we discussed exactly how to carry it out. In the meantime the story of Hamadera began to appear.

▼

As for what happened later, all the newspapers carried full reports of *that* scandal, so I'm sure you've read more than enough about it. I won't try to go into everything that took place in those last days—talking on and on like this has me too excited to be coherent anyway—

only there's a certain detail the newspapers missed, and that's the fact that the one who insisted we kill ourselves, and who made the final arrangements, was Mitsuko.

I think it was the day we learned about the letter Ume had stolen that Mitsuko brought over all my old letters, everything she had.

"It's too dangerous to leave these at my house," she declared.

"Shall I burn them?" I asked.

"No, no!" Mitsuko said quickly. "We can't tell how soon we may have to die, and I want to leave this whole record behind in place of a suicide note. Please, Sister, save all these along with the letters in your cabinet."

She told us to put our own things in order, and a few days later, around one o'clock on the afternoon of October 28, she came to us and said: "It's getting to be very difficult at home. I feel as if once I go back I'll never be let out again." She couldn't bear the thought of running away and then being pursued and caught, she said; better to die in our familiar bedroom.

Then we hung my portrait of Kannon on the wall over our beds, and together the three of us burned incense.

"If I'm watched over by my Kannon bodhisattva, I'll die happy," I said.

"After we're dead, I suppose they'll call this the 'Mitsuko Kannon,'" my husband put in. "Everybody will respect it, and we can rest in peace."

Let's nestle close, we agreed, one on either side of Mitsuko like the two bodhisattvas attending the Buddha—so close and intimate that we'd have no more jealous quarrels in our next lives. We joined the beds together and arranged three pillows side by side, with Mitsuko in the middle, and drank down that fatal medicine. . . .

▼

. . . What? Yes, it's true, somehow I wondered whether I might be the only one left alive. As soon as I woke up the next morning I wanted to follow them to the other world. But the thought came to me that my survival might not have been an accident; maybe I'd been deceived by them even in death. Wasn't leaving that packet of letters in my charge another clue? Perhaps they were afraid I might still come between them even after their love suicide! Ah. . . . (The widow Kakiuchi suddenly burst into tears.) If I hadn't had those suspicions, I couldn't have let myself go on living—and yet there's no use holding a grievance against the dead. Even now, rather than feeling bitter or resentful, whenever I think of Mitsuko I feel that old longing, that love. . . . Oh, please, forgive me all these tears. . . .

Junichirō Tanizaki was born in 1886 in Tokyo, where his family owned a printing establishment. He studied Japanese literature at Tokyo Imperial University, and his first published work, a one-act play, appeared in 1910 in a literary magazine he helped to found.
Tanizaki lived in the cosmopolitan Tokyo area until the earthquake of 1923, when he moved to the gentler and more cultivated Kyoto-Osaka region, the scene of his great novel The Makioka Sisters *(1943–48). There he became absorbed in the Japanese past and abandoned his superficial Westernization. All his most important works were written after 1923. Among them* Naomi *(1924),* Some Prefer Nettles *(1929),* Arrowroot *(1931),* Ashikari (The Reed Cutter) *(1932),* A Portrait of Shunkin *(1933),* The Secret History of the Lord of Musashi *(1935), several modern versions of* The Tale of Genji *(1941, 1954, and 1965),* The Makioka Sisters, Captain Shigemoto's Mother *(1949),* The Key *(1956), and* Diary of a Mad Old Man *(1961). By 1930 he had gained such renown that an edition of his complete works was published, and he received the Imperial Prize in Literature in 1949. Tanizaki died in 1965.*

A NOTE ON THE TYPE

This book was set in a digitized version of Janson. The hot-metal version of Janson was a recutting made direct from type cast from matrices long thought to have been made by the Dutchman Anton Janson, who was a practicing type founder in Leipzig during the years 1668–1687. However, it has been conclusively demonstrated that these types are actually the work of Nicholas Kis (1650–1702), a Hungarian, who most probably learned his trade from the master Dutch type founder Dirk Voskens. The type is an excellent example of the influential and sturdy Dutch types that prevailed in England up to the time William Caslon (1692–1766) developed his own incomparable designs from them.

Composed, printed, and bound by The Haddon Craftsmen, Scranton, Pennsylvania

Typography and binding design by Iris Weinstein

Yukio Mishima

THE SAILOR WHO FELL FROM GRACE WITH THE SEA

'Brilliantly prosed and composed...a major work of art'
Time

The Sailor Who Fell From Grace With the Sea tells of a band of savage thirteen-year-old boys who reject the adult world as illusory, hypocritical, and sentimental, and train themselves in a brutal callousness they call 'objectivity.' When the mother of one of them begins an affair with a ship's officer, he and his friends idealize the man at first; but it is not long before they conclude that he is in fact soft and romantic. They regard their disappointment in him as an act of betrayal on his part, and react violently.

'This novel is brilliant in the conciseness of its narrative'
The Nation

VINTAGE

Yukio Mishima

THE SOUND OF WAVES

'A work of art...altogether a joyous and lovely thing'
The New York Times

Set in a remote fishing village in Japan, *The Sound of Waves* is a timeless story of first love. It tells of Shinji, a young fisherman, and Hatsue, the beautiful daughter of the wealthiest man in the village. Shinji is entranced at the sight of Hatsue in the twilight on the beach, upon her return from another island, where she had been training to be a pearl diver. They fall in love, but must then endure the calumny and gossip of the villagers.

'Of such classic design its action might take place at any point across a thousand years'
San Francisco Chronicle

A SELECTED LIST OF CONTEMPORARY FICTION
AVAILABLE IN VINTAGE

☐	BIRDSONG	Sebastian Faulks	£6.99
☐	CHARLOTTE GRAY	Sebastian Faulks	£6.99
☐	MEMOIRS OF A GEISHA	Arthur Golden	£6.99
☐	HERE ON EARTH	Alice Hoffman	£6.99
☐	THE MAGUS	John Fowles	£7.99
☐	AMSTERDAM	Ian McEwan	£6.99
☐	ENDURING LOVE	Ian McEwan	£6.99
☐	THE SAILOR WHO FELL FROM GRACE WITH THE SEA	Yukio Mishima	£6.99
☐	THE SOUND OF WAVES	Yukio Mishima	£6.99
☐	BELOVED	Toni Morrison	£6.99
☐	PARADISE	Toni Morrison	£6.99
☐	AMERICAN PASTORAL	Philip Roth	£6.99
☐	THE MAKIOKA SISTERS	Junichirō Tanizaki	£6.99
☐	THE WAY I FOUND HER	Rose Tremain	£6.99
☐	A PATCHWORK PLANET	Anne Tyler	£6.99

* All Vintage books are available through mail order or from your local bookshop.

* Please send cheque/eurocheque/postal order (sterling only), Access, Visa, Mastercard, Diners Card, Switch or Amex:

☐☐☐☐☐☐☐☐☐☐☐☐☐☐☐☐

Expiry Date:_____Signature:_____

Please allow 75 pence per book for post and packing U.K.
Overseas customers please allow £1.00 per copy for post and packing.

ALL ORDERS TO:

Vintage Books, Books by Post, TBS Limited, The Book Service,
Colchester Road, Frating Green, Colchester, Essex CO7 7DW

NAME:_____

ADDRESS:_____

_____

_____

Please allow 28 days for delivery. Please tick box if you do not
wish to receive any additional information ☐
Prices and availability subject to change without notice.